THE DRUIDS OF BUSHMILLS

The Awakening

Suzy A Walker

CONTENTS

CHAPTER 1

When Ashton woke up that morning to her Mum yelling and bawling at her to get up, it felt like any other morning. Though it wasn't like any other morning. Today was the day that they were moving house. Ashton and her Mum lived on the outskirts of Belfast. They were moving to Bushmills to be closer to Ashton's Granny who was getting a bit past it. Although they only lived around an hour away, they didn't see each other often and they weren't close. From the little Ashton knew about her Granny, she knew that she and Ashton's Mum, Maureen didn't get along all that well, though she didn't know the reason why. She was looking forward to it though, Ashton never understood why they didn't see much of their extended family, she didn't have any siblings and had only ever met her Aunts, Uncles and cousins a handful of times, so it felt like they were a little isolated. She had never known her Dad or if he had any family, her Mum didn't seem to like to talk about him so she never really pushed the issue, she just guessed he was a wanker and didn't want to know her and thought it was his loss. She had few friends and found it hard to meet new people, probably mostly due to her massive case of foot in mouth disease. She was incapable of being dishonest, which most people took as her being rude and blunt, it didn't go down too well with people you'd just met when they said 'Hey its nice to meet you' and she replied 'Is it, I couldn't think of anything worse'. See what I mean? Massive case of foot in mouth disease. Anyway, fresh start and all that, maybe she would do a better job of being fake in her new life. Whilst she was most excited about having family near by she was almost just as excited about their new house. Ashton and her Mum lived in a tiny two bedroom, one bathroom apartment that was open plan, so their living room, dining room and kitchen was all one room and they'd never had a garden, just a shared patio area. She couldn't wait to have her own ensuite bathroom and a bit more space for privacy and also the garden for growing herbs and plants. Ashton loved gardening and growing things to add to her cooking. So today was the big day, they had pretty much packed everything into the moving van the day before. Most of their furniture was being put into storage as they'd have everything they needed in their new home.

After getting up and showering, Ashton went to see what needed done before they left. 'Morning Mum, what else needs done?'. Maureen replied, 'Good Morning Sweetie, not much, just our last few bits and pieces to be put in these boxes I've left over then we're good to go. I got you a fry from the cafe, some fuel for the journey.' I loved a good fry, sausages, beans, bacon, fried eggs and 3 hash browns. My Mum new me too well. 'Thanks Mum, I'll just eat this then I'll be good to go.'

It didn't bother me that I was leaving the only home I'd ever known. I was just glad to be getting out of here, so I didn't plan on looking back.

Within an hour we were on the road in the moving van. My Mum was a nervous driver so I drove us there, though I wish I hadn't of because she was an even more nervous passenger. 'You're going too fast', 'You're driving too close to the car in front', 'Watch that pot hole'. It was the longest hour of my life. I've never been so glad when I turned onto the road of our new home. Castlecat Road, it sounds made up I know, but its actually a real road in a real place, Google it. It's crazy to think that my family live somewhere called Castlecat Manor. Especially when you seen where we came from. It was set back from the main road, down a long winding country lane a mile long, surrounded by trees. As we got to the end of the lane it opened out onto a large courtyard area with a pond in the middle and beyond that, a huge gothic looking mansion with ivy covering the outer walls. I'd only been here a handful of times in my life but it never failed to take my breath away. I couldn't believe this was our new home. Set on 150 acres of land, with a castle on the grounds, with lots of outhouses and old buildings, I couldn't wait to explore it.

'Lets go inside, we can bring the rest of our things in later when Uncle Malcolm gets here', my Mum said breaking into my daydreams.

We went in the main front entrance, and into the hallway. It was as modern inside as it was gothic outside. It was absolutely the last thing you'd expect to see when you walked inside. A huge cut glass chandelier hung from the ceiling, the floors were covered in light grey herringbone porcelain wood effect tiles and the walls were panelled with textured wall paper in icy silver tones in between. What can I say, my Granny liked her bling. It was gorgeous, if not to my taste. To the left was the main sitting room and to the right was the large equally gawdy dining room. Two spiral staircases ran down either side of the hallway and at the end of the hallway there were entrances to the kitchen, two other sitting rooms, a games room, a sunroom, a bathroom, and 3 downstairs bedrooms all with en suites. A utility room and a walk in pantry also extended on from the kitchen and there was a door from the utility room which led to the large double 2 storey garage. While I was taking it all in my Aunt Emma appeared. 'Awk you're here, its so good to see you both, I can't believe you're actually here to stay, you better come through to the kitchen, Mummy has been cooking all morning, getting ready for you's coming'.

I smiled at her 'Its great to see you too Aunty Emma', she wrapped me in a warm hug then went to hug my Mum who looked mildly uncomfortable, two guesses where I got that from. I glanced over at my Mum quickly, a bit miffed that my Granny who is old and in need of looking after was in the kitchen cooking up a storm, she avoided my gaze.

We followed my Aunt Emma into the kitchen, it was a large space with a huge island in the middle which was modern yet had a homey feel. My Granny stood, white hair piled up in a bun on the top of her head, stirring a pot of soup. She lifted her head when we entered the room and broke into a huge grin. She didn't look old or sick or in need of looking after. 'Oh my God Ashton, I'm so happy you're here', she said while wrestling me into a bear hug.

'Hi Granny, long time no see, you're looking well', Ashton replied.

'As are you dear, albeit a little skinny.'

I snorted, I wished. You could always rely on Granny to make you feel good. When she finally released me, she went over to my Mum and gave her the same treatment, whilst my Mum stood awkwardly with her arms by her sides, the awkward apple doesn't fall far from the awkward tree. 'Hi Mummy', she breathed, she looked terrified though I had no idea why.

'Lets get you two something to eat, I've made chicken broth and beef stew with crusty loaf and some Victoria sponge cake and custard for dessert.'

'Thanks Granny, I'll have some Stew please, though I'll give dessert a miss, I already had a fry this morning'. I sat down at the large modern marble dining table with silver crushed velvet chairs with ornate silver legs. We all ate in relative silence, I couldn't help but feel like there was a bad atmosphere, although I'd no idea why, I was starting to feel pretty awkward when my Granny got up and scooped my bowl away and began rinsing it.

'Its ok Granny I'll do that, you should be taking it easy.' I said.

'Nonsense, I'm fine. I'm sure you want to go and chose your bedroom, there's two bedrooms free on this floor and any of the nine bedrooms on the first floor for you to chose from', she said.

'Thank you Granny, I'll go take a look upstairs, I'd quite like an upstairs bedroom after living in an apartment for so long'. I got up from the table and sneaked another glance at my Mum as I was leaving, she still looked terrified and tense. I walked back out into the hallway and up the left staircase.

When I reached the top of the spiral staircase I looked left and right along the long hallways, at the immaculate decor and the thick pile carpet. It reminded me of a hotel. I turned left and opened the first door I came to, the room was huge with a kingsized bed taking centre stage in the room, again all decorated in silver
hues. It was gorgeous but not the homey feel I was going for. I returned to the hallway and kept
going, the next few rooms decorated in a similar fashion, when I reached the last door on the left I
opened it to the corner room, this was the biggest room of all I had seen so far, it had panelling
similar to downstairs, and although it had silver textured paper like downstairs, it was offset by a
deep blue on the upper half and even on the ceiling, giving it a warm cosy feel. There was a massive
four poster bed made from white ash wood with an intricate silver and blue bedspread. To either
side of the bed was a white ash wood bedside cabinet and to the right was a large bookcase, already
partially filled with some books that I recognized, with a comfortable looking white ash wood armchair covered with more silver and blue fabric. To the right of that was the holy grail, my en suite
bathroom, complete with bathtub with jacuzzi jets and separate walk in shower. The walls were

tiled in stunning blue and white marble. I turned around and there was a dresser complete with
mirror, above which a big flat screen TV hung from the wall and to the right of that another door, I
walked over and opened the door to a huge walk in wardrobe, with enough hanging space to hold
the entire stock of TK Maxx, plus shelves for shoes and drawers for whatever else I needed. It was A-
mazing and I would never be able to fill it. Back outside of the dressing room, there were two windows, one on each outer wall, with curtains to match the silver and blue bedspread, under both windows were window seats made from the same white ash and with cushions to match the curtains and bedspread. It was perfect, as far as bedrooms were concerned, this was the one. I didn't even need to look at any of the other rooms. I turned on the TV and went and lay down on my new four poster bed and admired my new bedroom from it, this bedroom alone was half the size of our former
apartment.

'I see you've made yourself at home.' my Mum said waking me up. I groaned and rolled over to look
at her standing in the doorway. 'I must have drifted off, this bed is so comfortable, isn't this room
amazing.'

'Yes your Granny said she picked this room out especially for you, even the books on the
shelves are books that she knew you liked', my Mum said.

'That's really thoughtful. Mum I wanted to ask you something. I thought we were here to be near to Granny to help look after her, but she seems fit as a fiddle, am I missing something?'

My Mum seemed surprised at the question and avoided my gaze, then replied 'We will talk about this later, after we have unpacked and had something to eat, your Uncle Malcolm is here, he's going to help bring our stuff upstairs, my bedroom is at the opposite end of the hallway, I've taken the other corner room, lets go and help him.'

'Ok, just give me a minute,' I said, getting up from the bed, all the while wondering why my
Mum was being so secretive and avoiding my questions, and looking at me for that matter. She left
the room without another word.

I made my way downstairs after her. There was my Uncle Malcolm standing in the hallway, all 6 ft 5
of him, his floppy dark hair marred with more grey than the last time I seen him, with 3 boxes at his
feet, as soon as he seen me he run over and hugged me so hard he lifted me off my feet, 'I'm so glad
you're finally here sweetheart, where you belong.'

'Thanks Uncle Malcolm, you can put me down now though', he laughed and put me back on my feet.

'Sorry kiddo, I'm just excited to have you here'. I picked up a box and started to walk up the stairs.

'Where are you going', Uncle Malcolm asked.

'To my room' I replied.

He laughed and said 'I forgot how little time you've spent around here, you don't need to carry the box all the way up the stairs, use the dumbwaiter, there's one on the left side of the hallway that leads to outside your bedroom and one on the right side of the hallway that leads to your Mum's bedroom.'

'That's so cool, how did you know which bedrooms we'd chosen though.'

'Mum decorated a room especially for you, and I guessed your Mum had taken her old bedroom'.

We went to the dumb-waiter and put the three boxes inside, then I went upstairs to retrieve them and take them into my bedroom. I wondered how my Granny would know I'd chose the room she'd

decorated for me. I guess she knew me better than I thought. We continued bringing boxes in and

unpacking them until the removal van was completely empty. It was later than expected when we

finished. By the time I washed up and went downstairs in search of food it was 7.45 in the evening. I walked into the kitchen where my Granny, Mum, Auntie Emma and Uncle Malcolm and another younger man sat surrounded by plates of food, seemingly doing more whispering than eating, when they were alerted to my presence they all guiltily looked at me and quickly shut up.

'Hey, what's going on, if I didn't know any better I'd say you were all talking about me.'

'Of course we're not talking about you Ashton', my Mum said rather sharply.

'Calm down it was a joke Mum.' She just looked down at her barely touched plate.

'Here, I made gammon, roast beef, roast potatoes, mash, broccoli, carrots and cauliflower, load your plate up and get something to eat, before your Uncle Malcolm eats it all.' Granny joked to diffuse the awkward silence.

'Thanks Granny, I'm starving'. I made myself a plate and sat down to eat. 'I'm going to go to the job centre tomorrow and start looking for jobs, I'm hoping to get something quite quickly so I can afford to get a car soon.' I said.

'Oh there's no need to rush dear, you need more time to settle in, we have everything you need here, you can use one of my cars.' Granny replied.

'Well, I'd at least like to get out and about and learn my surroundings a bit better, is there even a local shop around here? Or a library or a gym?'

'I can take you', interjected the man I didn't know, I turned to look at him, taking him in for the first time, he looked to be around the same age as me, mid 20's with startlingly white skin with contrasting black hair that just covered his ears, and green eyes the colour of peridot.

'I don't go on outings with strangers,' I retorted, then realised what I'd said as soon as the words had left my mouth.

He laughed long and loud, 'I'm Adam, and you do know me, we used to play together every day when we were kids when you lived here.'

'I didn't live here.' I replied.

'Oh my mistake, it must have been some other bratty five year old that stuck a pencil in my ear and perforated my eardrum.'

I burst out laughing, 'It must have been because I have no memory of that whatsoever and I have never lived here.'

His face turned serious, 'She doesn't know?'

Granny interjected, 'Now's not the time Adam, let Ashton get settled in first.'

'Now's not the time for what? What am I missing here?' I said annoyance sounding in my voice, at the fact that everyone had been acting strange all day and my Granny seemed perfectly fine, which was the whole reason for us uprooting our whole lives and coming here in the first place, not that I had minded that part if I'm honest anyway.

Everyone fell silent. 'Great, keep your secrets, I'm going to bed.' I said as I got up and emptied my half eaten plate in the bin, rinsed my plate and stormed out of the room and up to my bedroom.

I was nearly 25 years old for God's sake, it was my birthday next week, yet I was being treated like a
child and being left out of the loop. My Mum had barely spoken two words from we got here and
had been acting shady all day, avoiding looking at me, avoiding answering my questions and now
Granny was doing the same. What was Adam even talking about, I didn't know him, I had never lived
here. I had always lived in Belfast, with very little contact with my extended family, or anyone for
that matter. A knock at the door broke me out of my internal rant, it was my Mum. 'I'm sorry
sweetheart, there's things I need to tell you, but I wanted to give you time to settle in, no one is purposely evading your questions, they are just allowing me the time to tell you myself.'

'Tell me what yourself Mum, what's going on?' I said.

'Can you just give me a day or two until we're more settled and I will tell you everything, I promise.'

'Sure that's great, you've got a secret, that clearly involves me and everyone but me knows and they're all giving me weird looks and avoiding answering my questions, and Granny seems perfectly fine even though she's supposed to be sick, and apparently I lived here but have no knowledge of it, but I'll just hold on for another couple of days until you decide you can be bothered to tell me whatever this big secret is.' I seethe.

'I understand you're upset, but I really wasn't expecting you find out so soon and there are some
important things I need to do first. I'm not trying to avoid your questions. I just need a bit of time,
can you please just be patient.'

'I suppose I don't have much other choice do I?' I replied dejectedly.

'No, I suppose you don't, be patient, I promise I will tell you everything soon sweetheart.'

'Fine, good night, close the door on your way out'.

My Mum sighed and got up to leave, when she reached the door, she turned back to look at me and said, 'I've only ever tried to do what's best for you.'

I softened, 'I know that Mum, good night.'

'Good night.' she said quietly and closed the door.

I found it hard to stay angry with my Mum, but really what kind of bullshit was this. I am not a patient person, it will drive me crazy waiting for days to find out whatever this big secret is and I would no doubt struggle to sleep tonight now, with a million ideas and possibilities running through my head. Like why would I not remember living here, if I lived here when I was 5 I would have some memory of that, wouldn't I? Though I suppose its possible that I wouldn't. But then, what about Granny being sick? I haven't seen her in about 5 years, I was told she was getting old and was unwell and needed help, but if anything she seemed younger than the last time I seen her and vibrant as ever, she didn't seem like someone who needed help. ARRRGHHH! Fuck it, I'm going to get in my jacuzzi bath and try to relax or I'd never get any sleep tonight. I ran my bath and got into the warm bubbly water and closed my eyes and tried to clear my mind, but it was impossible. 'Why do you look constipated?' a voice said.

'Aaaarrrrrrrrrrrrrrrrrrrghhhhhhhhhhhhhhhh', I screamed and jumped up out the bath completely naked staring right at Adam. 'Get out of here right now, what do you think you're doing you pervert'.

He held both his hands up in front of his eyes and took a step back, 'Sorry, I knocked your door and there was no answer, so I was afraid you'd tried to escape and let myself in, I wasn't expecting you to be in the bath with the door open, then I seen you lying there making that strange face, you were perfectly covered by all the bubbles, well until you screamed like a banshee
and jumped out of the bath. I promise I tried not to look.'

'TRIED not to look? Get OUT!!! I will kill you.' I screamed.

'Sorry, I'm going I'm going, but I really am sorry, I feel like we haven't got off to the
best start, it was never my intention to upset or offend you in anyway or invade your privacy.' Adam
said all the while still covering his eyes and making me feel guilty for yelling at him and threatening
to kill him.

'Close the door.' I barked.

He obediently closed the bathroom door while still covering his eyes with one hand.

'Let me get dressed, I'll be out in a minute' I said slightly more calmly now that my naked body wasn't on display.

'Ok, I'll be waiting', he said.

I got dried and dressed and tried to mentally calm myself. Then I opened the bedroom door to Adam
lying sprawled out on my bed like he owned it, with his head propped up with his arm, as if he was
on display for me. 'Hey Sweet Cheeks,' he said.

'In the name of God and all that is Holy, Adam if you
want to live you will get off my fucking bed right now.' I said completely losing the calm I had

mustered.

'You still have a fiery temper then, good to know'.

'GET UP'. I growled through gritted teeth.

'Ok, ok, I'm up, I'm just having a little fun with you'. He got up and walked to one of the seats and I walked over and sat on the bed and faced him.

'So you were going to apologise, get on with it then.'

Adam burst out laughing and as much as I wanted to stay angry, I couldn't hold back a laugh when I seen how much he was cracking up, so both of us laughed until there were tears rolling down our cheeks. I could hardly get a breath. Finally we both stopped laughing long enough for one of us to get a word in, it was Adam. 'I'm sorry, I didn't mean to cause any problems at dinner.
I didn't realise that you weren't in the loop about certain things, clearly no one kept me in the loop about you not being in the loop. I just assumed you would remember me from when we were kids, your Mum and my Mum were the best of friends, so naturally so were you and I, well until the pencil incident I mentioned earlier at least.' I laughed again. Adam was funny without even trying to be.

'Ok apology sort of accepted, but only because you're trying to guilt me about the pencil incident, which I have no recollection of by the way, tell me everything you know and I may think about possibly forgiving you for all the trauma you've caused me today at some point in the very distant future.'

It was Adams turn to laugh now. 'Oh thank you for considering forgiving me, but really that's all I
know. You lived here until we were around 6, not long after the

pencil incident and then you and
your Mum moved away and broke my tiny heart. My Mum told
me a couple of months ago you guys were moving back here
soon, so I came today, mostly for your Granny's
cooking, and also to invite you guys over for dinner, I thought
you might have remembered me, I
find it strange that you don't. I have plenty of memories, besides
the pencil.'

'When I think back, my first memory of this place was when I
was around eight or nine. I guess I had to have been here before
then, I never really thought it was unusual before now. I still
don't understand what the need for secrecy is though, surely
that's not all you know. What were you all whispering about
when I came down for dinner?' I asked.

'Oh that, we were just talking about your birthday party next
week, I wasn't supposed to tell you about that so if you tell
anyone I told you I'll totally deny it ever happened.' Adam
grinned at me.

'Really? That was it? Maybe I'm being paranoid, I thought
everyone was acting totally weird and avoiding my questions
today, and that's what its all about. But what about my Granny?
My Mum told me we needed to move here because Granny was
sick and needed looking after, yet if anything I'd say she looks
even better than the last time I seen her. Do you know what's
wrong with her?' I asked.

Adam looked uncomfortable, 'As far as I'm aware there's nothing
wrong with Granny, but I don't know why anyone would tell you
something so awful if it isn't true, so maybe only family know.'

'Why do you look so shifty Adam? I feel like there's something
you're leaving out.' I probed.

14

'I just don't like the thought of your Granny being sick, shes like a Granny to me too. Anyway its getting late, my Mum will be wondering what has taken me so long. I can come back tomorrow and show you the sights, if you're up for an outing with a stranger.' He said sticking his tongue out. I laughed, 'Yeah sure why not, just not too early.' 'See you tomorrow Ashton.' he said as he ducked out the door.

I flopped down on my bed, my head still reeling from such a strange day. Nothing was as I expected it to be here. Were my family really just organising a birthday party for me, is that the only reason for everyone avoiding my questions. I knew I wasn't going to get any sleep any time soon so I decided to go in search of the library, that I knew was on this floor. I love reading but I hadn't unpacked any of my books yet. The library was on the other side of the hallway about half way down. It was a cosy room, untouched by my Granny's bling. An old stone fireplace was set into the centre of the room with armchairs dotted around the place and a large table by the window to the right of the room, with reading lights and chairs placed around it. The rest of the room was covered in floor to ceiling bookcases. This just might be my favourite room in the house, aside from my bedroom. I looked along the rows upon rows of books. Some of the books looked so old, I wondered where my Granny got them from. They seemed to be arranged into categories. I loved reading about history but fantasy fiction was my guilty pleasure and the biggest section of books here seemed to be on witchcraft, these seemed to be the oldest books in the library, leather bound, with yellow weathered paper. I picked one of the books up off the shelf, there was no title on the book but a picture of a tree was engraved into the leather cover. I took the book over to the table and turned one of the reading lights on. I opened the front cover only to find the first page was blank. I turned to the next page, and it was the same, confused I started flicking through the pages only to find that they were all blank. This was the most bizarre thing I'd ever seen, an ancient looking book that looked well used, the cover was worn, the pages were fragile, yet there was not a single thing written inside it. Giving up on it, I went and placed it back on the bookshelf and started browsing through the other books. I picked up a more modern looking book, titled a History of Druidism in Ireland and took it back to one of the comfy arm chairs and began to read.

I woke up in the arm chair with no idea where I was. It took me a few moments to remember. I slowly got up, stiff from sleeping in the chair and walked over to place the book on the table to pick up again later. I wondered what time it was. It was still dark outside when I looked out the window. I was about to leave to go back to my room when 6 cloaked figures walked past outside in the smaller courtyard at the back of the house and down through the entry between the sunroom and the garage. In a panic I ran to my room, shoved my feet into my shoes and ran down the spiral staircase and through the back of the house and out kitchen door and ran down the entry following in their direction. In that moment I realised I'd lost all my senses and I didn't even have a weapon or my phone to call for help. I decided I'd just sneak quietly and hopefully go unnoticed and see what they were up to, then I could creep away and call for help. I put my back flat to the entry wall and moved slowly until I got to the end, I couldn't see anything other than a dim light in the furthest outhouse. I ran to the old stone building, and peered quickly through the window before moving out of sight, there was no one in there but the back door was open, the light that I could see was coming from beyond the door. I needed to know what was going on, so I opened the solid wooden front door of the outhouse, cringing when it creaked on its hinges, then thanked God when it closed silently behind me, and crept up to the open back door to peer beyond it. In the field beyond was a large opening with five stone structures arranged in a circle, they were shaped nearly like people only much taller and attached to each was a flaming sconce, but most surprisingly, in front of each sconce were the hooded figures I'd seen, with one standing in the middle in front of a large blackthorn tree. What the fuck? Is that 'Uncle Malcolm?', oh shit I just said that out loud, I hid myself again, but I was too late.

'In the name of Christ, Ashton, what are you doing here?', Uncle Malcolm swore.

'What am I doing here? More like what are you doing here, creeping about in the dark in cloaks like cult members about to do a sacrifice, what the hell is going on?' I yelled back, completely horrified at what I was witnessing.

'Ashton calm down', it was my Mums voice now.

'Let me talk to her', Granny interjected.

'Oh for fuck sake, not you too, have you's all gone stark raving fucking mad, what kind of nut cases am I related to, what are you doing here Mum, have you lost your freaking marbles, am I supposed to pretend this is normal behaviour, are you's doing cosplay or something, because as embarassing as that would be it is preferable to the alternative, that you've lost your fucking mind', I yelled back, not even caring that I just swore in front of my Granny.

At the same time my Granny and Uncle Malcolm burst out laughing, as my Mum said, 'Watch your language Ashton'.

'Are you kidding me right now? Does someone want to tell me whats going on before I call the mental hospital to see if they have a ward free for all you crazies,' I retorted, frustrated now that no one was answering me. Aunt Emma and another woman I didn't recognise stepped forward then, Aunt Emma spoke in a soothing voice 'Why don't we go back to the house and get a cup of tea and we can talk about it there.' It was then that I noticed my Uncle Mark behind them, he nodded sheepishly at me, 'I'm officially emancipating myself from this family', I said to thin air as they all walked past me back to the house. I walked along behind them, looking at them all in their ridiculous clokes when a fit of giggles came over me. Maybe this is why Mum wanted nothing to do with them all, they were all insane and it was catching so she wanted to stay far, far away so it wouldn't rub off on her, as apparently it didn't take long to be infected. I laughed again, cracking myself up. Granny turned back to look at me and grinned, that just did it for me, I laughed until I choked on my own saliva then I started coughing and retching in a really ladylike way as I stumbled the rest of the way to the house. I was so giddy I felt high.

When we got inside, Granny put the kettle on, Mum bustled about beside her getting cups and sugar and seemingly doing anything to keep busy and avoid looking at me, Aunt Emma, Uncle Malcolm, Uncle Mark and the woman I didn't know all sat down at the table and looked at me expectantly. I reluctantly pulled the chair out far away from the table and then sat down and crossed my arms and said, 'Explain yourselves then'.

'Have a bit of patience Ashton, let us get the tea ready first', Granny said.

'I have been here for less than 24 hours, and so far I have discovered I have been lied to in the worst possible way, and brought here under false pretenses, then I'm told that I lived here before, which I have no memory of, which is totally bizarre that first of all I don't remember and second of all even if I didn't remember, no one in my entire life since then has mentioned. Not only that but you're all being secretive and avoiding my questions, then Mum tells me she will explain everything but I just need to BE PATIENT, there's that word again, for a couple of days until she sorts some "important stuff" out, and NOW I wake up in the middle of the freaking night to find you all frolicking about the garden in the grim reapers robes. No one on this earth is that patient, and you must think I was born yesterday if you think I believe that this is all about my surprise birthday party. So spit it out, what the hell is going on?'

'Ok you have a point, but it's a long and complicated story and you may find some of it difficult to hear and to believe, so maybe its best to get that part over with and just show you.' Granny said.

'Show me what?' I said as Granny clicked her finger and thumb together and a small flame shot out of her thumb like it was a lighter.

I laughed, 'Cool trick Granny, how did you do it?'.

'Its not a trick Ashton its magic', she replied. I laughed again and looked around at everyone else's somber faces.

'Oook, I just remembered I have a phone call to make, I'm just going to go and lock myself in my room while I make it and you guys all stay here until I get back,' I said getting up from my chair mumbling under my breath 'Or until the men in white coats come'. I began to walk out of the room, when my Mum yelled, 'Ashton, damn it will you just sit down and listen, we aren't crazy.'

'Try telling me that when you aren't dressed like a Jedi Mum', I quipped back.

'That's it, I've had it', she shouted, in the voice that always made me do what I was told when I was a kid, but I wasn't a kid anymore, so I shouted back, 'That makes two of us!', then tried to storm out of the room when a gust of wind came out of nowhere and knocked me on my ass. It's just as well I had plenty of cushioning or that would have hurt. I stood and turned, about to ask what the hell was that but when I looked at my Mum she was standing with her hands outstretched and it seemed as though wind was swirling around her, blowing her hair all around her like she was in some sort of shampoo advert, the blinds and the curtains were moving, as was the table cloth, I stood for a second dumbstruck with my mouth hanging open, completely forgetting that I meant to speak. My Mum stared back at me, furious, seriously she was furious with me. I came to my senses, 'Mum, how are you doing this', her shoulders sagged and she dropped her hands and the wind stopped in an instant. 'Magic', she whispered, 'That's the big secret, would you please just sit down and listen.' She was serious, I could tell by the look on her face. I walked back over to my chair and sat down. 'I'm sitting and I'm listening'. My Mum walked over to the table and pulled out her own chair and sat down and stared at me blankly.

'Maybe I should start', Granny said after a moment, when it seemed like Mum wasn't going to say anything. But Mum straightened up in her chair and sighed then said,
'No it should come from me. Ashton our family are descendants of Druids, some people think of us as witches and although in some ways we are similar, we are also very different. We possess magic, that is enhanced by the nature that surrounds us. We have always been the protectors of this land, in the past, power hungry necromancers have tried to claim it to raise their dead.' My Mum paused and took a deep breath before she spoke again, 'One of those necromancers was your Father.' I had been sitting listening intently until that point, humouring them whilst wondering when someone was going to tell me that the whole thing was an elaborate prank, but I had never heard my Mum mention my Dad voluntarily, EVER. 'What are you saying Mum? You can't be serious, none of this is true.' I whined.

'I'm sorry sweetheart, I didn't want to tell you this way, but it's the truth and there's more I need to tell you.'

'How do you expect me to believe this, it's total make believe, like a story in the books I read. Magic isn't real, necromancers? Also not real. Have you listened to yourself?' I said, getting annoyed again.

'Try something for me,' Mum said quickly, 'Stand up and close your eyes, take a deep breath and hold it.'

'Look I don't know what you're trying to do Mum but this is ridiculous,' I countered.

'Please just trust me Ashton, you've trusted me your whole life until now, what's a few more minutes.'

'Fine,' I said, standing and closing my eyes. I sucked in a deep breath and held it like she asked.

'Good, now feel that point in your centre, where you're holding the breath and imagine pushing it out slowly to your fingers and beyond them.'

I did as she asked feeling silly, knowing everyone was watching me without even opening my eyes, I tried not to think about it and focused on that feeling in my belly and I pulled it back up through my chest and down my arms to my hands, I had the strangest sensation, like I could feel elastic stretching from the point where I held my breath, I opened my eyes and let it go and that's when all hell broke loose, it felt like the elastic snapped back inside me, like lightning struck right there in Granny's kitchen, in fact I'm nearly sure it did, the window cracked, flame ran up the curtains, the ground shook and a gust of wind knocked me off my feet again and that's the last thing I remember.

CHAPTER 2

I woke, in my bed to the sunlight pouring through the open curtains. I must have forgot to close them last night, I was exhausted and felt sore all over, I rolled over and away from the light determined to go back to sleep, but as I rolled over I noticed movement by the armchair, there was someone sitting in it. I screamed and rolled back the way I came until I landed on the floor tangled in my quilt but I still managed to get my feet on the ground, I moved quickly backwards until without looking I came to the window seat and I had no option but to fall back onto it on my butt. It was then I realised who was sitting there, it was Adam and he was laughing his ass off. 'What are you doing here? Come to watch me while I sleep, creep? I said snidely, while I tried to untangle myself from my quilt. That just made him laugh even more.

'More like watching you while you were unconscious. Did anyone ever tell you, you sleep like the dead,' he laughed again. 'I opened the curtains to try and wake you because I was genuinely too afraid for my life to try and shake you awake.' After untangling myself from my quilt, I walked over to the bed and threw a pillow at him which hit him with a satisfying thump.

'You're right to be afraid. What are you doing here anyway?' I said, sitting back down on my bed minus the quilt which was still bunched up on the floor by the window seat.

'Forgotten already? I'm supposed to be taking you out to show you all the scenery and fields that Bushmills has to offer.' Adam said with a smirk. He got up and went over to my walk in wardrobe, he grabbed a jeans and a cream aran jumper and threw them at me, 'Hurry up and put these on so we can go.' he said.

'I'm only awake, give me a minute.'

'I'll go wait downstairs, come find me when you're ready.' he said already leaving.

I got a quick shower, still loving my en suite. It was only whilst I was in the shower I woke up enough to remember what had happened last night and wondered if it was some crazy dream and also how I got into bed. It must have been a dream, nothing else made sense, as vivid as it seemed, so I put it to the back of my mind. Once I was ready I headed downstairs, the smell of food calling me from the kitchen. I walked in and there was Adam, stuffing his face with what looked like a sausage and bacon bap and he was sitting beside the woman I seen with Auntie Emma last night in my dream. That was weird, if it was a dream how did I dream up the exact woman that was sitting here in my Granny's kitchen. Dumbstruck I opened my big mouth without thinking, 'You were in my dream' I said looking at the woman. Adam looked up from his bacon sandwich, laughed and subsequently choked, ha serves him right, I smirked at him. Just then my Granny came out of the utility, drying her hands on a hand towel, 'Morning Ashton, how are you feeling after last nights ordeal?' she said.

At her words my bubble burst, I had tried to play it off as a weird dream, but there was no point in lying to myself. I could still feel the stretchy elastic band right at my belly button waiting to spring or rather stretch into action. I walked over and sat down at the table, noticing for the first time the plates of fried eggs, sausages, bacon and baps sitting on the table, usually I would dive in, but I'd suddenly lost my appetite, as good as it smelt. I looked up at Granny, 'It was real wasn't it.' I whispered.

'Yes dear, it was real, as real as my broken window and singed curtains,' she said waving her hand in the direction of the window.

'Oh my God, I did that, did I do that? How did I do that?' I rambled. Adam and the blonde lady beside him and my Granny all laughed at once.

'Which question would you like me to answer first?' Granny chittered, 'Yes you did that, you done it with your magic, you're a druid like all of us with a little bit of extra spice thrown in. I don't think anyone expected you to do what you did last night, you're powerful and that's with your magic bound.' she said like she was pondering something.

'With my what now? My magic bound? How can I use my magic if my magic is bound? How did it get bound? And hang on a second, what do you mean a druid like all of us, is Adam a Druid too?' I said glaring at Adam. 'And who the hell is this woman and why are you telling all my secrets in front of her?' I said catching her eye.

She laughed, Adam's jaw dropped, then she spoke, 'Hi Ashton, I'm Adam's Mum, Leona, your Mum and I have been best friends since we were kids, Adam and I live just down the road, I'm glad to see you haven't changed a bit, you were just as cheeky when you were six and I'm so happy to have you back with us where you belong. You're like family to us.' she said smiling widely at me.

'Um thanks, sorry, I didn't mean to be rude, but I thought you were in my dream last night, before I realised it wasn't a dream and then you were here again today and I just realised I really wanted to know who you are. Its eh nice to meet you, well again. Sorry I don't remember much from before, well actually I don't remember anything.' I said rambling again.

'I know sweetheart, don't worry, it will come back to you after the ceremony.'

'What ceremony?' I asked. 'I'll let your Granny explain that.' Leona said, then she got up and said 'Well me and Adam better be off, we will come back later.' she smiled at me again.

'But I thought Adam and I were going out.' I said looking at him getting up from his chair.

He shrugged and said 'We'll do that tomorrow, promise. It seems like you've plenty to be getting on with here, see you later.' and off he went abandoning me to my fate.

'Eat.' Granny said shoving a plate with a sausage bap loaded with tomato ketchup under my nose, it smelt good, so I decided to dig in.

'I'm sorry about how last night went. I thought I we could do with a chance to talk alone.' Granny began.

I interrupted 'So you sent Adam to wake me because you knew he was the one I was least likely to throw something at. I did by the way, throw something at him I mean'.

Granny chuckled, 'You figured that out did you. Despite the circumstances I'm so glad your finally here.' Granny gave my arm a squeeze.

'I know, I am too, glad to be here I mean.' I smiled, then took a bite of my sausage bap. 'Anyway, I wanted a chance to talk to you alone, because this whole situation is very upsetting for your

Mum and she tends to get emotional and shout'. I rolled my eyes knowingly. Granny went on, 'When your Mum was 22 she met a man, your father. She thought they were in love, she fell pregnant with you and then found out that he was a necromancer. He had only seduced to her for information. Necromancers have been around for as long as Druids. Their power whilst similar to our own is darker, they can temporarily reanimate corpses, or raise the dead as if they had never died. Well the more powerful necromancers can, most don't have that sort of power anymore. Some powerful necromancers draw on their own power to raise the dead or increase their life span, with little to no consequences. Others, the majority of them, must work in numbers to achieve such things, or draw power from nature or their surroundings, with devastating consequences. Necromancers and druids, worked closely together until around 200 years ago. Druids have always been protectors and necromancers once were too. There were many powerful necromancers, they raised armies of reanimated corpses to win battles, they could help heal the sick and they prolonged life where they could. But after the typhus epidemic in the early 1800's many of the powerful necromancers who rushed to the aid of the sick, contracted typhus themselves and too weak to heal themselves they perished. The powerful necromancers who were left didn't want to risk themselves to help the sick any longer and instead went into hiding. Around 65000 people died. Some of the less powerful necromancers banded together to try and bring back their leaders, but as they didn't have the power, they pulled power from nature, causing what we now know as the Irish potato famine, killing many more people, to bring back few of their own. When the Druids realised what was happening, we stepped in to stop them, by protecting our lands and nature against them. It caused an all out war with the necromancers and many on both sides were killed. You see, Druids like necromancers have their own power, however our power is enhanced by nature and our ancestors like I told you. It is a careful balance of give and take. We give offerings to our ancestors, we nourish and protect nature and our lands and in turn our ancestors and the lands allow us to draw power from it, but we only take what we need. The old necromancers were very similar to us in this way, they just had a different kind of power with different abilities. But after the typhus epidemic, with mostly the weaker necromancers remaining, they rewrote the rules so to speak, they began taking without replenishing the power that they took, they drained the island dry in a bid to make themselves more powerful to bring back their leaders and then again so they could defeat us, their own ancestors cut them off. We had many losses as did they. We would not take from the land that they had already drained dry, so we could only rely on our own power and gifts of power from our ancestors. With both of our numbers decimated, we went away to regroup, however we have been enemies ever since. With the necromancers rearing their heads every now and again to try and seize power or control of our lands, where our ancestors are buried. Our ancestors will only provide help to us, their own ancestors, however the necromancers believe they have found a solution to this, again trying to take power that doesn't belong to them. Its no longer as easy for necromancers to draw power from nature because of modern civilisation, so they reside in the countryside however most of the areas they can draw power from are inhabited and protected by Druids. Running out of options, the necromancers started drawing power from the living, many missing persons are down to them. They also prey on easy targets, like the sick and elderly and drain their life force bit by bit. They are the lowest of the low, only the worst type of people would prey on the weak and elderly like this, to feed their addiction to their imagined power. Lately there have been murmurings that the necromancers have found a way to draw power from our Druidic ancestors. I hope it's not true, but I know better than to leave anything to chance, so we must prepare for the worst possible outcome and be ready to fight against the necromancers when the time comes. '

'How can this be true? How can people not know about Druids and necromancers?' I asked finally getting a chance to get a word in. I had way too many questions to even know where to start.

'People believe what they want to believe. If something is too far fetched or out there, people will choose to believe the rational explanation.' Granny replied. Then she added softly, 'I'm sure you would like to know more about your Father, I don't know as much about him as I would like, I just know that your Mum was devastated when she discovered who he really was. Not wanting to break the connection he had formed with her, he told her that he only hid who he was because he had wanted to get to know her and then he had fell in love with her so he couldn't tell her that he was a necromancer because he knew that she despised them. He knew about you though, the night that your Mum went to tell him that she was pregnant, was the night that she found out he was a necromancer. They used to meet up at Bushfoot Strand in Portballintrae. When your Mum arrived he was waiting on the beach and she told him she was pregnant, but it was a set up, he had brought other necromancers there with him. There was a confrontation and your Mum had to fight then run and hide to get away. She arrived home in the middle of the night, hysterical, unable to tell anyone what had happened, traumatised by her ordeal. She spent the best part of a week in bed. No one knew that she was pregnant or that she had been seeing someone. When she finally told me the truth, she was terrified that the family would disown her, or that I would be disappointed in her, but the truth is my heart broke for her, and you my unborn grandchild, that she had been so callously mislead and that you would grow up without a Father around. I never blamed your Mum for what had happened, but I think she blamed herself. Eventually after a few weeks, your Father showed up, he told your Mum that he loved her and he wanted to run away to raise the baby where you would all be safe, but she didn't trust that he was telling her the truth and thought that he was trying to use her for his own gain amongst the necromancers. He plead with her and told her that he had not told anyone about the pregnancy, but she refused to go with him and told him she never wanted to see him again. So instead he swore to her, to protect you both and to prove that he really did love her, that he would never tell a soul about you and that he would stay away and would not interfere in your life in anyway, unless she ever needed him. So he left and she never heard from him again, just like he promised.'

'I always knew talking about my Dad made Mum sad so I gave up asking a long time ago, I didn't want to know him if he made my Mum feel like that. But do you ever wonder if maybe he was telling the truth, maybe he really did love her.' I pondered.

'If you knew the necromancers like I do dear, you wouldn't believe that, they are ruthless. They will do anything in the pursuit of power. But even if he did love her as you suggested, it could never work out. With your mixed blood line, the necromancers would have tried to use you to gain access to our ancestors and our land. He could not take you to live amongst the necromancers and he could not live here amongst us as he was a necromancer and he had proven by lying to your Mum for so long that he couldn't be trusted, the only other option was to run away and and then they would always have been looking over their shoulders, which is no life for a child. We put plans in place, as we did not take his word that he would not tell anyone about your existence, we are not killers, as much as I would have liked to get my hands on him and throttle him, that is not our way, so we reached out to our ancestors and asked them help us strengthen the protection on our land. If a necromancer comes within a mile of our land their power will be diminished. So you lived here, safely until you were six years old. Between the ages of four and six Druids begin to show signs of their abilities. Most if not all Druids, have a specific ability, either earth, air, fire or water. I'm sure you can guess which ability I have.'

'Fire.' I whispered, then added, 'and Mum has air ability'.

'You're right on both counts. Now can you guess which yours is?'

'Erm, is it lightning? I'm sure I seen lightning before your window cracked and the curtains went on fire,' I grimaced, 'actually lightning isn't an ability so that must mean I'm air, like Mum'.

'Yes and no. Ashton, you are the only known Druid alive with all 4 abilities.' Granny paused, 'But that's not all, you seem to have gained some abilities from your Fathers lineage. When you were 5, you had an imaginary friend, well so we thought, it turned out you could talk to the dead and your imaginary friend was in actual fact my Granny.'

'NO WAY, how is that even possible?'

'Some necromancers can only sense spirits, some powerful necromancers can communicate with them, but very few can both see and communicate with them. You could do that at five years old.' She went on, 'When you were six, we were in the fields beyond the outhouses having a picnic with your Mum, Leona and Adam were there too. You found a dead mouse in the field and you bawled your eyes out, you wrapped it in a napkin and brought it back to the house to give it a funeral but instead you brought it back to life.'

'Oh my GOD. So am I a necromancer? And if I am does that make me evil like them?' I babbled, I had the tendency to ask way too many questions when I'm panicking.

Granny laughed, 'No dear, you are not evil, nor have you ever been, you don't have an evil bone in your body. You are just a dolly mixture of both Druid and Necromancer and powerful at that. After the incident with the mouse, we were afraid of any one finding out that you had necromancer blood and what you could do. You are possibly the most powerful necromancer in over 200 years. We had to bind your magic to keep you safe. Initially your Mother and I tried to do it ourselves, but the binding didn't last, with your power being heightened here on our lands. Instead we had to use our entire Grove to cast the binding, but we also had to take your memories to keep you safe, that's when your Mum decided that you would be safer away from Druids and Necromancers, so she took you to the city to try and keep you safe and to keep the binding in place. But that could only last so long, a Druid reaches their full power when they turn 25, and with your power, the binding will never hold you. There is a ceremony we have to do on the eve of your birthday, after the ceremony your memories should begin to return and the binding will slowly unravel.'

'Holy shit, I'm like a superhero. But Granny, what's a Grove?' I wondered out loud. Granny burst out laughing, 'Oh Ashton, I have missed you. A Grove is what a group of Druids is called, like a coven of witches.'

'That's so awesome, so am I a part of the Grove now?' I asked, like an eager kid.

'Yes, after your ceremony you will be a part of the Grove.'

'I just can't believe this is all real. I've lived such a normal, albeit isolated life, but I lived in Belfast for God's sake, I went to school, I went to university, I lived in a bloody tiny apartment and not one single magical thing has happened to me in my life until I arrived here. Well that I remember anyway. But it's insane that this whole other magical world exists and I had absolutely no clue. At first I felt silly for even entertaining the notion that this could be true, but there's no other explanation unless you're all liars and/or insane and I've inherited that wonky family gene too.'

Granny laughed again, 'No wonky genes here. Come on, I want to show you something.'

I got up and followed Granny out the back to the out buildings and beyond them where I had discovered them all at the stone circle the night before. Was that really only last night, I thought. This shit was crazy. This place was kind of awesome though, now I could see it in the day light, the stone circle really looked like stone people placed around the blackthorn tree which also kind of looked like a person.

Granny spoke, 'This stone circle represents our ancestors, it has been here for hundreds of years. This is a place of great power as this is the burial ground of many of our ancestors. We hold our ceremonies here to draw strength from our ancestors. This is where your ceremony will be held in a couple of days. We came last night to ask our ancestors for help strengthening the protections here. We cannot wait any longer though, it must be done tonight, and now that you know everything you can help if you want to.'

'Do I have to wear one of those daft robes?'

'Yes, you have to wear one of those daft robes.' Granny replied dryly.

'Ok then I'm in, I always loved fancy dress.' I grinned back at Granny.

CHAPTER 3

I was in my room getting ready when Adam just waltzed in like he owned the place. This was getting to be a habit. 'Hey, who says you can just walk in here whenever you feel like it.' I grumbled.

'Hi to you too. I just brought your robe up, but if you like I can take it back downstairs and let you get it yourself.'

'Well maybe you could knock the door in future at least.'

'Sure I could but then I might miss out on the opportunity of seeing you in the nude again.' He grinned.

'Adam, I will gut you.' I growled.

'Ok, I'll knock, calm down, I was just joking with you', he said holding his hands up whilst backing away, all the while holding the robe on the hanger.

'Ok fine, is that for me?' I asked. He handed the robe to me. 'Why do you wear these things? What is the point?' I wondered.

'It's a sign of respect to our ancestors and for our traditions.'

'I don't know anything about our ancestors or traditions, I've been kept in the dark my whole life remember? I still can't get my head around all this. I just keep thinking this can't be real.'

Adam walked over and sat down in my armchair and said softly, 'I don't agree with them taking your memories, I didn't know. I knew they took you away to keep you safe, but I was so young when you moved away that they didn't tell me much. It's a lot to take in, you haven't even been here a day and your whole life has changed. Give yourself a bit of time, you will love it here, I'm sure.'

'Yeah I guess so, I'm just glad to be close to family, it's always been kind of lonely just me and Mum, I never understood why we didn't come to visit more, it all makes sense now.' I said, then I had a thought, 'Adam, what kind of magic do you have?'

'Why do you want to know?' he asked.

'Stop being annoying and just answer the question.'

'You literally don't possess a single bit of patience do you,? I have air magic like your Mum, and like you I suppose.'

'Awesome, so you could teach me?' I said excitedly.

'Nope, nope and did I say nope? Because it's not going to happen!' Adam said shaking his head.

'Awk Adam, wwwhhhhyyy?' I whined.

'Because, like I just mentioned, you don't have an ounce of patience and you're impulsive, you also have more than one type of magic and you wouldn't listen to a bloody word I say, or you would listen and then you would do what you wanted anyway. My Mum told me about what happened the other night, she said you drew on all 4 of your abilities at once and nearly blew up your Granny's kitchen and I'd rather not get blown to bits.' he finally took a breath.

I burst out laughing, 'So what you're saying is you're scared of me. That's ok, I understand, I'll ask someone more experienced'.

'You do that, I'm not biting.' he replied with a smirk.

'Ah well, it was worth a try.' I laughed.

'Let's go, everyone will wonder what's taking us so long.' Adam said turning to leave. I followed after him, feeling both nervous and excited. I didn't really know what to expect and no one had filled me in on much. My Mum had just came to see me earlier to apologise about last night and see how I was. So here I was, thrown in at the deep end yet again.

When we got to the kitchen everyone was there plus several people I didn't recognise. There was Mum, Granny, Aunt Emma, Leona, Uncle Malcolm, Uncle Mark, plus me and Adam. Everyone was too busy talking to notice me and Adam arrive, all except for one man who looked similar in age to us, as soon as we walked in he looked up and stared right at me as if in shock, the second his gaze fell on mine, I got an electric shock sensation at the bottom of my spine, goosebumps broke out on my arms and I gasped, noticing my reaction, he quickly looked away. Adam who was walking in front of me, turned and gave me a quizzical look. I wondered who the hell that was and why he looked at me like that and what was with my embarassing reaction, I could feel my face heat in shame. I shrugged at Adam and averted my gaze. I sneaked another glance at him, and he was staring at me again, the two women he was talking to now noticing his reaction to me, I could feel my face go purple this time and turned my back on them and walked over to the fridge, opened it and stuck my head in hoping it would cool it down, when Granny came up beside me and scared the bejesus out of me. 'What are you doing with your head in the fridge dear?'

'Erm, I er was just looking for something cold to drink, thirsty.' I mumbled. I grabbed a can of coke and closed the fridge door. 'So when do we start? I've no idea what I'm supposed to be doing.' I tried to act casual.

'Just follow our lead and you'll be fine, there's nothing to worry about, you'll see. We should be starting shortly. Your robe looks good on you'. she said.

'Thanks Granny.'

We all headed out not long after that to the stone circle where I had discovered them the night before.

Granny, Mum, Aunt Emma, Leona and Uncle Mark all took their places in front of the large stone stone statues after lighting their sconces and Uncle Malcolm stood in front of the Blackthorn tree again. Granny told me to stand beside her in between the stones that her and my Mum were standing at, Aunt Emma stood at the stone on the other side of Granny, with Uncle Mark on the other side of her and Leona on the other side of Uncle Mark and Mum making up the circle. Adam stood between his Mum and Uncle Mark. The man I seen stood between Uncle Mark and Aunt Emma and the two women he was with or talking to before stood together between Aunt Emma and Granny. Another older man appeared that I hadn't seen before and he stood on the other side of the Blackthorn tree to Uncle Malcolm. When everyone was in place the man spoke, 'If everyone is ready, we will begin calling on our ancestors.'

Everyone nodded in unison, except for me because I didn't know what the fuck I was doing, until I realised that he was staring at me waiting for my response, so I cleared my throat, shuffled awkwardly and nodded too.

Suddenly it seemed eerie standing here by only the light of the flames and the moon, under these ancient statues, the hairs on the backs of my arms began to prick up, and I started to get a little bit freaked out and then the older man began to speak. 'We gather, the descendants of the ancients, with reverence and thanks, we call upon our ancestors, to aid us in shielding these lands, against those who wish to do us harm. May their spirits infuse us with strength and unity, protecting the lands and those within those lands that we hold dear. Hear us, our mighty ancestors and lend your boundless power to our cause, so mote it be.' He nodded again and everyone began to chant 'So mote it be', so I followed their lead just like Granny said and then everyone started to join hands. The second the final hands joined the wind picked up, it blew my hair in my eyes and I raised my hand in Granny's about to swipe it away when she shook her head, so I pulled it back, then a voice spoke but it wasn't coming from anyone I could see, 'So mote it be', and then just like that every single flame went out. I panicked in the pitch black, I could only see the distant lights coming from the house through the windows of the outbuilding, I still had a hold of Granny and Mums hand and tightened my grip, I was afraid to speak and break the spell but Mum spoke first, 'Are you ok Ashton?'

'Yes I think so,' I squeaked, 'Was that supposed to happen? With the flames and the creepy voice I mean.'

'The wind and the flames going out was pretty typical, but what creepy voice are you talking about? Do you mean David? I wouldn't call his voice creepy.' Mum replied.

'Who's David? It was more of a female voice, she said 'so mote it be' but I didn't see who said it.'

'David is the High Priest of our Grove, he began the ceremony. We all said that, Ashton.' my Mum said dryly.

'I don't think it came from any of us, I thought it was maybe one of our ancestors letting us know that they had heard us and were willing to help. How do we know they heard us? I mean anyone with air magic could have caused that gust of wind and made the flames go out. I was expecting something a bit more concrete and spectacular if I'm honest.'

'My God Ashton, what do you think this is, a TV show? It's real life. Our ancestor's always send us a sign, but they can only use the gifts they already possessed in life to show us that they heard us, hence the gust of wind. No one in the circle could have caused the gust of wind because all of our hands were joined, so we would have felt it if someone who was part of the circle used their magic as it would have fed through all of us.' Mum said exasperatedly.

'Well excuse me for not knowing, considering you stole my memories and kept of all this from me for my entire life so I can only jump to my own conclusions. Then you brought me here tonight with no idea of what to expect.' I raged. When I looked up everyone was staring at me. Including the stranger who had been staring at me earlier. I sucked in a breath to calm myself down, from not only my annoyance but the fact that he was staring at me again. My Mum spoke again drawing my attention back to her, 'I'm sorry, you're right, you weren't to know and that's something we will fix and soon, after your ceremony.' I nodded back at her, I wasn't really annoyed at my Mum about taking my memories, I could understand why she did what she did even if I didn't totally agree with it, but she also needed to have some patience with me, she couldn't expect me to know everything on day 1 without telling me a thing.

We all headed back into the house. Once there Granny put together a feast for everyone. I was just stuffing my face with multiple cocktail sausage rolls when she nudged me, I turned to look at her and the man who I discovered was called David was standing next to her, 'Ashton, this is my friend David, he's the High Priest of our Grove.'

'It's a pleasure to finally meet you Ashton, I've heard so much about you. I will be helping with your ceremony in a couple of days, if that's ok with you.' he smiled sincerely. He was similar in age to Granny with strikingly unusual silver coloured eyes that crinkled at the corners when he smiled. I couldn't help but smile back at him, 'Nice to meet you too David, unfortunately I haven't heard a thing about you before tonight because I have no memories, but you're more than welcome to help with my ceremony if you can change that.' He laughed, 'I will certainly try my best.'

Everyone continued chatting and eating and every now and again I sneaked peeks at the man who had been staring at me earlier, and every time I did, he was staring at me again. It was starting to get a bit weird. I was just about to go and talk to him and ask why he kept staring at me, when Adam came up to me and said, 'Do you want to get out of here? Mia and Sophia said they're going to Bushfoot Strand, there's a bunch of other people there, if you want to come and meet them.' I thought about it for a second then said, 'Sure why not, I'm not tired yet.'

'Cool, they're going to give us a lift, so lets raid your Granny's fridge and see what booze she has.' he grinned.

'Or you could just ask,' I said, then called out, 'Granny, we're going to go to Bushfoot Strand. Have you got any booze we could borrow?' I asked.

'Of course dear, there's some tins of apple cider in the fridge, or there's prosecco and wine, take whatever you want.' My Granny was the best.

'Thanks Granny,' I said gratefully. Me and Adam set to work loading a couple of bags with way more alcohol than we could drink ourselves, then said our goodbyes, took our robes off and went out and got into the back of Mia's red Ford Focus.

'Hi, I'm Ashton by the way, thanks for the lift.' I said awkwardly introducing myself since no one else seemed bothered to do it.

'We know who you are.' Sophia said. 'Everyone knows who you are.' Mia added.

'Well it's nice to officially meet you both,' I said self consciously.

'Yeah sure, you too.' Mia replied dryly. I really got the impression

I wasn't welcome here though I had no idea why because I'd never met these girls or done anything on them. Hopefully I was just being paranoid. I wasn't good with new people.

'So what are we waiting for?' I asked, unsure of myself and my position in this social setting.

'Oh we're just waiting on Lucas.' Sophia said.

Just then Lucas aka Mr Creepy Starer got into the car beside me and squished me in the middle between him and Adam. Up close he smelt good, and he looked even better. I immediately got goosebumps again and shivered all the while still staring at him. I caught myself and inwardly cringed at my obvious reaction to him. Adam rescued me by speaking, 'You cold? Shift over and I'll keep you warm,' he said putting his arm possessively around my shoulders.

'I'm fine,' I said, 'You never miss an opportunity do you Adam.'

He laughed and said 'God loves a trier'. I looked up to see Mia and Sophia glaring daggers at me through the rearview mirror.

Lucas spoke then drawing my full attention back to him, 'Hi Ashton, I'm Lucas. If your cold you can take my jacket. It tends to be windy down at the beach.' I couldn't help but just stare at him for a second, he was gorgeous, he had the brightest blue eyes I'd seen, sandy coloured hair mixed with strands of white blond and a deep golden tan. His eyes were transfixed on mine and mine on his. When I realised I was staring yet again I said, 'Good to meet you. Thanks but I'll be ok especially after a few drinks.' Besides I was warm enough tucked in between him and Adam.

It was less than a 10 minute car journey to Bushfoot Strand. Mia and Sophia and the boys chatted on the way there, I kept mostly quiet and stared out the window, taking in the scenery. I wondered how my Mum used to get here when she met up with my Dad.

Once we were there, we grabbed our drinks and a few blankets from the boot of the car and walked down to the beach. There were people here already, with a large fire lit and a couple of smaller ones and there was a portable speaker blasting out tunes. I got as close to the big fire as I could without accidentally igniting, and sat on one of the blankets and basked in the heat while Adam got us plastic cups for our drinks and poured me a prosecco. I definitely wasn't cold now. Adam sat on one blanket with me while the two girls Mia and Sohpia sat on another, seemingly annoyed at the seating arrangements if their scowls were anything to go by. Lucas had made a beeline for some guys he knew as soon as the car had pulled up. A girl with long straight fiery red hair to her waist and pale white skin dotted with freckles approached us wearing an off the shoulder cami top with skinny jeans and white flat sandals, she was stunning and I couldn't help but feel a little inferior in my scruffy jeans and jumper and my high tops. She knelt down on our blanket and said 'Hi guys,' with a bright smile while leaning in to hug Adam, then 'Hi Ashton, I'm so glad you're here,' and instantly pulled me into a hug too, I was a bit taken aback by this warm welcome and hug from a perfect stranger. 'Wow, you're friendly,' I said, then realised that was probably a bit rude, 'Sorry I didn't mean it like that.' She waved her hand and laughed 'No worries, I'm a hugger. It's a fun way to make people feel uncomfortable.' Just then she looked up at Mia and Sophia and said, 'Hey do you guys want a hug too.' They both just glared at her. She held her hand up and mock whispered, 'They're the friendly bunch really.' I laughed, I liked her. 'So tell me everything about yourself, I probably know most of it because Adam has talked about you non stop for months since he knew you were coming back here.' Adam punched her lightly on the shoulder, 'Cheers for that Fiona.' So that was her name Fiona. 'Do you want a drink?' he said clearly to change the subject. 'Sure I'll have some of that prosecco if you're offering.' she said holding her hand out, Adam poured her a plastic cup of prosecco and handed it to her.

'Thanks, so back to you Ashton, how are you finding it here so far? Your Granny is the best isn't she. Now we're friends I'll be able to just drop in to see you and get fed. Her cooking is amazing.' I laughed again, I couldn't get a word in, I thought I was chatty. As the evening went on I met more and more people, I couldn't remember half of their names, the prosecco wasn't helping in that department either. I was disappointed that I didn't see Lucas anymore either, when did that happen? I was missing the creepy starer. He had maybe gone home. I was getting a bit tipsy, Fiona and I were just dancing to a song we both liked and then out of the blue there was a piercing scream coming from further down the beach. It was hard to see that far down with just the moonlight and fires for light, but it looked as if someone was running towards us, as she got closer I could see that it was Mia. Fiona, Adam and I ran down the beach to meet her, 'What's wrong Mia, what's happened?' I asked. '

Tears were running down her face and she was shaking, 'Someone got Sophia, I think it was the necromancers, there was a cadaver and it grabbed me and she was trying to beat him off me when someone came up behind her and smoke wrapped around her and then Sophia and the cadaver and the necromancer all disappeared, just into thin air. I've never seen anything like it, necromancers don't have that sort of power.' So that answered a question I was asking myself earlier, did everyone at this party know about Druids and necromancers? It appears so. Fiona put her arm around Mia and said 'It's ok, we're going to get her back, if it's the necromancers the best place to go is Ashton's house, her Granny and David will know what to do.' She said comfortingly.

'But what if they bring her back here and we've left?' Mia sobbed. By this point there was a large crowd gathered around. I spotted Lucus, I couldn't help but wonder where he had got to, I hadn't seen him for at least 2 hours. 'I doubt if someone has went to so much trouble to get her, that they're just going to bring her back,' I said without thinking. Mia glowered at me.

'Ashton's right.' Adam said, 'Let's go back to the car and go to Ashton's house.' It was 1.30 in the morning, I wondered if my Granny would mind us coming and waking her up, but it was an emergency so I'm sure she would forgive me.

We gathered our stuff and walked back to the car, it struck me that Mia was the only one not drinking and she was in no fit state to drive. When we got there Lucas was already at the car, he must have gone on ahead. 'Mia why don't you get in the passenger seat, I will drive us back, I haven't been drinking,' he said. Mia momentarily forgot how torn up she was about Sophia disappearing and smiled sweetly at him, obviously delighted, she must have realised this herself and instantly put her head down and started sniffling again. Lucas walked around and opened the car door for her then went and got into the drivers side while me, Adam and Fiona all got into the back seat, I guess she was getting a ride with us. We were all quiet on the short drive back to Granny's house, or my house, I should get used to saying. When we pulled up in the courtyard outside, every light in the house seemed to be on. I guess I needn't have worried about waking everyone.

We got out of the car and walked into the main hallway and found the glitzy cut glass chandelier my Granny loved, smashed to pieces in the middle of the floor, 'Oh my God, where's Mum and Granny?' I panicked running into the kitchen to see if they were still there. The kitchen was as bad as the hallway, covered in broken glass and plates, food all over the floor, The Granny's Kitchen, Granny's Rules plaque my Granny kept proudly on the wall was split into 2 pieces. I breathed a sigh of relief when I seen Granny, leaning over David, cleaning a cut on his forehead. Mum looked like she'd been trailed through a hedge backwards, her hair was coming loose from her pony tail, she had dark streaks on her face and there was a large singed hole in the sleeve of her blouse. Everyone else looked to be in similar states of disarray but otherwise ok, it looked like David had came out of it the worst. 'What the hell happened here?' I asked, everyone filing into the kitchen behind me. Granny looked up surprised to see me. 'Oh thank God you're alright Ashton, the necromancers attacked us, they know about you Ashton, they were looking for you, we've been betrayed. They used wraiths in the attack to get around our protections.'

'They attacked Mia and Sophia on the beach, they've taken Sophia. Mia tell them what you told us.' I said.

Mia started forward unsteady on her feet. Granny said, 'Why don't you sit down and tell us Mia,' taking her by the arm and leading her to a chair, then added, 'Adam get her a glass of water'. No one argued with Granny.

Mia sniffled as Adam handed her the glass of water and took a sip before speaking, 'I was attacked on the beach by a cadaver, they grabbed me and Sophia tried to fight them off when a necromancer came up behind her and a this smoky shadow wrapped itself around her and they all just disappeared into the thin air.'

'It has to have been the wraiths.' Granny said. 'Only they could do that, the necromancers must be controlling them.'

'How are we going to get Sophia back? Or where are they likely to have taken her?' I asked.

'They have a base at Dunluce Castle ruins. I don't know where else they could have taken her.' Granny said.

'So when are we leaving?' I said.

'Ashton, we would likely be walking into a trap, if they came here for you that is probably exactly what they want and are expecting you to do. We need to think about this.' It was Lucas that spoke surprising me.

'Lucas is right,' Adam said, 'we need a plan, and one that doesn't involve you, we need to keep you safe.'

'Hold on a second, first of all, I'm the only one who gets a say in where I go, though I get that it's likely to be a trap. They might also expect you to leave me here, so they can get to me more easily whilst everyone's gone. So I say we all stay together, or anyone that wants to goes and anyone doesn't want to stays. As for a plan, how about we use me as bait. They don't know that we came back here, they won't be expecting us to go so soon, but if we make them think we followed them from the beach to get Sophia back we might catch them off guard. All of us that were at Bushfoot Strand will go in first, the rest of you wait for 15 minutes then follow us there. I will try and distract them and then the rest of you can come in and rescue us all.' I said with a grin.

'Ashton you have lost it, if you think I'm going to let you put yourself at risk like this.' Mum said angrily. 'I know you think this is exciting, but its dangerous.'

'Mum I'm perfectly aware of the danger, especially the danger that Sophia might be in because of me if we don't go, so unless any one has any better ideas, we need to hurry this up and get going.' I said.

Everyone fell silent, contemplating my plan and trying to think of a better one.

'I'm going with you,' Adam finally said and broke the silence.

'So am I.' Lucas agreed.

'It's my sister, I'm going.' Mia said.

'I'm in too.' said Fiona.

'Let's get going then.' I said.

'Hang on Ashton, you need weapons, come to the library'. Mum said leaving no room for argument.

We followed her to the library. She spoke to me on the way, 'Usually Druids do not like to use weapons, as we have our power, but we don't know what you're walking into and you have no training or experience.' We walked into the library and to the far back wall, Mum pulled one of the book cases forward and then slid it across over the bookcase beside like a sliding door revealing a small secret room, weapons covered the walls and there were 3 chests placed around the outside of the room. My Mum walked over to the far wall and took a pair of throwing stars and handed them to me, she grabbed a belt from one of the chests and told me to put it on, I did as I was told and put the throwing stars into it, they were gorgeous, silver with a blue stone inlaid into the handle, then she handed me a sheath for my ankle and another short knife like a Sgian Dubh with a black leather handle and silver blade with and intricate design engraved where the handle met the blade. Everyone else helped themselves to weapons.

Once we were back downstairs my Mum, Granny, Auntie Emma, Uncle Mark and Uncle Malcolm walked us to the door. 'Adam, look after her.' my Mum said. I snorted, 'Who's going to look after him?' Adam shot me a glare.

'Go now, try to find Sophia, we will leave in 15 minutes.' Mum said and pulled me into a quick hug. 'Stop fussing,' I said, 'we'll be fine.'

We got into the car and they waved us off.

Lucas was driving again, with Mia in the passenger seat and me and Adam and Fiona in the back. Fiona was the first to speak, 'This was not how I seen tonight going.'

'You and me both.' I said. 'So when we get there, I think me and

Mia should go in alone first. They will expect Mia to be looking for her sister and me to give myself up in exchange for Sophia. If the rest of you hold back for a few minutes you might be able to get in unnoticed and get to Sophia to help her escape. Are you up for that Mia?'

'Yes, I don't have much choice, they have my sister.' she replied.

'I know there's no point in arguing with you, but I just want it to be heard that I think you're insane. You're going in there with no training, you've used your magic once - that you can remember and that went so well, you nearly blew up your Granny's house then you passed out, you have a couple of weapons you've never used before and you're walking into the necromancer's base which you've never been to before which is exactly what they want you to do.'

I grinned at him, 'Did you get that out of your system?' He rolled his eyes thinking I couldn't see him in the darkness of the car. Fiona laughed, 'It does sound a bit insane when you put it like that, but sometimes the simplest plans are the best, we didn't have much time to come up with another one since they had Sophia anyway.'

Everyone fell silent after that in a world of their own thinking about what we were about to do.

CHAPTER 4

Lucas pulled us up into a layby about 200 meters down the road from the Castle, I could see it in the distance, although all that was left of it was ruins, you could see how majestic the cliff top stone castle once was. There were wall's but no ceilings, instead they were covered with white tarpaulin.

Me and Mia got out of the car, the others agreed to follow in a few minutes. The cold air was biting at this time of night or morning should I say, even in the summer. After walking most of the way in silence I spoke to Mia, 'Almost there, I've been meaning to ask, what kind of power do you have.'

'I have water magic, which will be useful since we're so close to the sea.'

'Ok, we're almost there, it looks like the only entrance we can use is over the bridge down that way,' I said pointing. It was a modern wooden structure that the necromancers had obviously added at some point.

Mia just nodded, she was maybe getting nervous now that we were here I thought to myself, or she was more than likely worried about her sister.

As we turned to walk down the pathway the bridge was on I heard a noise, like feet shuffling on the ground, I looked around but couldn't see anything. I thought about using the torch on my phone that was tucked into my pocket but that would only alert the necromancers to my presence. Although that was kind of the point. It was too quiet here. I was sure that the necromancers were lying in wait, I didn't like the feeling that someone could jump out on us at any second. In a split second decision, I yelled at the top of my voice, 'We're here, you were looking for me and now I'm here, so you can let Sophia go.' Mia shushed me with an incredulous look on her face as if to say are you stupid. Then all at once, light erupted around the place, sconces lit on walls and four necromancers came, two from either side of the bridge and two took Mia by the arms and the other two took my arms. 'No need to get handsy, I'm here of my own free will.' I said. I tried to get a good look at them but their faces were covered to just below their eyes with black scarves and they were wearing wool hats as well along black combat trousers and combat boots, they reminded me more of military men than supernatural beings. They didn't speak a word, they just lead us down a winding pathway, deeper into the labyrinth that was the ruint castle. I hadn't really thought this through, it was going to be harder for anyone to find us than I initially thought.

When we were near one of the castle walls closest to the cliffs edge, they took us into a room covered in tarp, with three men inside, and Sophia. She smiled when we entered, she didn't look like she needed rescued. Suddenly it dawned on me, this whole thing was a trap to get to me. Sophia and Mia must have been in on this together. But then, if they planned this, why did the necromancers go to Granny's house to look for me. Something didn't add up.

'Sophia, you're ok,' Mia sobbed. She tried to move towards her sister but was held back by her captors. 'What's going on Sophia?' Mia asked. The penny dropped, Mia didn't know what Sophia had done.

Sophia spat, 'I was getting this freak out of the way, no one wants her here, well apart from the necromancers. She's too powerful, she is only going to bring trouble to the Druids, proven by the fact that she has only been here just over a day and is already causing trouble.'

'But I don't understand how you even became involved with necromancers in the first place. I thought you'd been taken, or were maybe even dead.' Mia said anger and disbelief creeping into her tone.

'This is John, my boyfriend.' Sophia said, holding her arm out to the closest of the 3 men with a grin. They all looked the same with those scarves round their faces and their hats on.

'How could you do this Sophia? You're a traitor. I didn't like her at first either but this is too far. She came here for you to save you. I'm ashamed of you.' Mia said disgusted.

'More fool her then,' Sophia replied.

'Enough of this, we have to take her to him' John stepped forward and reached out a hand towards me. I'd had enough of this shit, I stamped on left goon's foot and elbowed him in the face, then donkey kicked right goon in the balls causing them both to fall to the floor, then closed my eyes and summoned my magic up from my belly button through my body and down my arms faster than I had before and pushed my arms out in front of me and blasted John right through the wall behind him, the debris from the blast hit Sophia and the other two goons taking them down, Sophia cried out. Holy shit, I can't believe I just did that, but no time to thing about how awesome I am. I had to help Mia, she had used my distraction as an opportunity to break free from one of her goons, the other still had a tight grip on her arm and she was struggling to lose him, without thinking I pulled one of my throwing stars from my belt right at his arm and unbelievably hit my target first time, he cried out and let go of her. I crossed the room towards her, realising I was unsteady on my feet and a bit woozy, I grabbed her by the arm, 'Lets get out of here fast before they recover.'

'But what about Sophia,' she cried.

'I think Sophia has chosen her side and I for one would like to get the hell out of here while I'm still breathing, lets go.' I said pulling at her arm again. She took one last glance around the room and at her sister, then nodded and reluctantly came with me. We ran back up the way we thought we came, but it was dark and the place was like a maze, we'd no idea where we were going. We heard a commotion, obviously Sophia and John alerting the others to our escape, suddenly there were necromancer commando guys everywhere, we ducked and hid where we could but it was impossible to keep moving without being seen, we had ended up turning back on ourselves at some point and were close to the sea side of the castle again. We heard the necromancers coming and I grabbed Mia and pulled her flat to the ground with me below the opening of a low window frame made of crumbling stone, I sucked in a breath and held it, hoping to not be seen or heard or that would be the end of us. Suddenly there was shouting and flashes of light up ahead of us, then screams. What the hell was going on? We were never going to get out of here by lying down and hiding, so I made another stupid split second decision and jumped up from where I lay on the ground, 'Mia, we can't stay here, lets go' I whispered frantically. Just as I stepped out from around the crumbling stone wall a necromancer nearly ran into me, 'oh shi--' I tried to say as the necromancer grabbed me, with one arm around my neck and his other hand grabbed my arm and he turned me so my back was to him, it was then I realised I felt the chill of sharp metal at my neck, he had a knife. Faster than I could even see what had happened, he was threw back by what seemed like a tidal wave, that kept crashing over and over him so every time he tried to get up he was threw back down, Mia saved me. 'Thanks,' I said surprised, 'Come on.' As we ran back uphill the way we came, we could see people fighting all around us, thank God our rescuers had arrived, Mum, Granny, Uncle Malcolm, Auntie Emma, Uncle Mark, Leona, David, Fiona, Adam and Lucas were all there fighting off the necromancers. Mia blasted another necromancer from behind with her water magic and we side stepped around him to reach the others. 'Oh Ashton, thank God you're alright, wheres Sophia?' My Granny asked at the same time setting a necromancer on fire and he rolled down the hill away from us. Mia spoke before I got the chance, 'Sophia's our traitor. We need to get out of here.' Granny looked back at her sharply and nodded. We joined the fight but I was too tired to use my magic, so instead I punched, kicked, bit and hair pulled my way through any necromancers that came near me. There seemed to be more of us than there were necromancers left and the ones that remained were retreating. After dispatching a necromancer with her air magic, my Mum clasped her cool hand on my arm and half dragged me up the hill back towards the bridge, everyone followed. We went as fast as we could, afraid that more necromancers would come. When we got back to the road, we ran as fast as we could with the little energy we had left back to the layby where there were now 3 cars parked. Mia and Lucas got in the front of Mia's car and me Fiona and Adam got in the back, we all sat in silence for a minute catching our breaths. The others had gone and got into their own cars. 'Everyone good?' Lucas said as he started Mia's car and turned the headlights on and pulled out onto the road, one of the other cars pulled out behind us.

'Good's a bit of a stretch, but we're alive.' Adam said. We all laughed.

Lucas put on his indicator to turn left before we reached as far as the Castle, but just as he was slowing down to turn, someone in all black came running out onto the road in front of the car with their hands held up as if in surrender. Lucus slowed more, 'What should I do?' he asked.

'Run him the fuck over and get out of here.' I said ferociously.

'It looks like he wants to tell us something.' Adam said.

'I don't care what he wants to tell us, its likely another bloody trap, just drive Lucas.' I said.

'I agree.' It was Mia who spoke quietly.

'Wait, there's 5 of us and one of him, lets find out what he has to say.' Fiona was the voice of reason.

'Fine, but if I die, I'm going to get a necromancer to bring me back to haunt you all.' I said.

We had stopped by this point, the other cars stopped behind us too, probably curious as to what we were doing. Lucas pressed the button on the electric window and put it half way down and waited. The necromancer approached, we all stiffened in the car, I pulled on the stretchy elastic in my belly holding it taught ready to strike if needed. He stopped about a meter away from the car. 'I have a message for Ashton,' he spoke first.

'Get on with it then.' I said.

'Gavin want's you to know that he didn't give you up, he has asked that you meet with him. He wouldn't even share the time or location with me, he will get in touch with you tomorrow and wants you to consider meeting with him. We aren't all evil like some people would have you believe. I have to go, just think about meeting with him, please.' he turned and ran before any of us had the sense to speak.

'Who the hell's Gavin?' Adam asked.

'I have no idea.' I said quietly thinking about who I thought it might be.

Lucas started to drive and the cars behind followed. We were all exhausted, from the fight. I was starting to feel aches in places I didn't even realise I'd hurt. No on spoke much on the way back.

We arrived back first and got out of the car as Granny, David, Mum and Uncle Malcolm pulled up in their car, Aunt Emma, Uncle Mark and Leona, pulled up behind them in their car. We all trudged into the house, I'd forgotten what a mess it was in from the necromancers earlier attack.

Granny spoke as she entered, 'Everyone stay here tonight, we have plenty of spare bedrooms. We are safer together anyway.'

Me and Mum showed everyone to the spare rooms upstairs. Once everyone was settled in their own room, I headed back to mine, so tired that I thought about forgoing the shower I so desperately needed, but one look at myself in the mirror soon stopped that idea. My hair was plastered to my head with sweat, I'd dirt on my face and clothes and scratches on my arms and one on my jaw. I peeled my disgusting clothes off and put them in the basket in the bathroom and decided to get a shower as it would be faster. Everywhere hurt, my cuts stung and my head was sore and I felt weaker than I had ever felt before. I was sure that I would pass out as soon as my head hit the pillow. Once showered, I put on my cosiest pajamas and climbed into bed ready for sleep. As I lay there though, I couldn't help but think about everything that had happened over the last few days. Then my mind turned to Gavin, I wondered was he my Dad and if I should go and meet him, I was sure I wasn't supposed to trust him, but I was also pretty certain that I would have to make up my own mind about that, which meant meeting him. I'm not sure how Mum would feel about that. I had wanted to ask her if it was him but I was way too tired to have that conversation tonight so I thought I would ask her tomorrow. It technically already was tomorrow. I grabbed my phone from the bedside cabinet where I had left it charging and groaned, it was 4.12am, I set it back down. I need to go to sleep. I pulled my blanket right up to my chin and closed my eyes. My eyebrow got itchy so I freed my hand and scratched it then rolled onto my side and lay on my scratched arm, ok not that side then so I rolled onto my other side. My wet hair that I hadn't bothered drying tickled my face so I shoved it out of the way and snuggled back into my quilt and lay peacefully - for 2 whole freaking seconds, now I was too warm, I kicked my blanket off. As exhausted as I was, I knew I wasn't going to sleep, I was too wired, too much had happened in a short space of time and my brain wasn't ready to switch off. I let out a huff and got up, immediately making the decision to go to the library to find a book to read. I remembered the book on a History of Druidism and it now had new meaning, I'd began to read it when Druidism wasn't real, well wasn't real to me yet. Now I knew different. I left my room barefoot in my cosy pajamas and walked down the hallway and opened the door to the library. One of the reading lamps was already on and Lucas was bent over a book. He looked up, surprised to see me. 'Sorry, I couldn't sleep, so I remembered the library was here, I hope that's ok. Are you alright?' he asked. Suddenly I felt self concious in my fluffy llama pajamas, then realised I wasn't the only one wearing pajamas, lucas was wearing loose fitting shorts and t-shirt pajamas, though at least his were plain, no llamas in sight.

'That's ok, it's not my house. Yes, I'm fine, I couldn't sleep either. What are you reading?'

'I found this book with the symbol for the tree of life on the cover, but all the pages are empty. I was wondering if it's spelled, I was thinking of testing my theory out when you came in.' He raised his eyebrows as if to say do you want to.

'What's the tree of life?' I replied.

His eyebrows shot up again, this time in surprise. But he replied, 'In Druidism the Tree of Life can represent many things, it protects the land surrounding it, and can be a doorway to the spirit world, it is also a place of power where we can easily reach our ancestors. Some even believe the tree is one of our ancestors, I'm not sure what I think about that though. Most of the texts written about the tree of life are hundreds of years old. I'm not sure if it still applies to the modern world. The blackthorn tree here on Castlecat Manor, is the only tree of life throughout the whole of Ireland, North and South, that's why many of our ceremonies are held here, because it's a place of power.'

'Wow that's pretty cool. So what was the theory you were going to test out?' I asked intrigued now.

'Well I was thinking that maybe this book was spelled with blood magic. Although Druids don't usually do blood magic, its more of a necromancer thing, in the past it was much more common. So I had the idea that a drop of blood might reveal the contents of this book. Should we try?' he asked, then added, 'Or do you mind if I try? I've never seen a book like this before, though I've heard of them.'

'Sure why not,' I replied, excited to see if it would work.

'Do you have anything sharp? A pin or a knife?'. I looked around but couldn't see anything that could be useful.

'I have a knife in my room, why don't we go get it, we can try it there.' I said without thinking.

He smirked, 'Sure lets go.' My face went purple.
'Don't get any ideas.' I said dryly.

He followed me out of the library and down the hall to my room. When we got there I lifted the ankle sheath and knife from where I'd left it lying on the floor and handed it to him. I went and sat on my bed with my legs crossed and watched as he perched on the edge of the armchair seat with the book balanced on his knees. He got the knife and pushed the tip of it into the end of his index finger until a bead of dark red blood appeared. He held his finger over the tree on the cover of the book and a droplet fell. We sat waiting for something to happen, and when it didn't, I got up from the bed and walked over to look at the book. As I leaned over my long damp blonde hair brushed against Lucas' arm and I heard his intake of breath as I opened the cover and started flipping through the pages, but they were still blank. 'Maybe we have to say magic words or something.' I said.

Lucas burst out laughing, 'Why don't you try? I hear abrakadabra is a good one.' he teased.

'Well how the fuck am I supposed to know, I've known I'm a Druid for less than 48 hours.' I fumed.

'Ok, you're right I'm sorry.' Lucas backtracked, still trying to hold back a smile. 'Maybe you could try.' he suggested.

'Why would it work for me if it won't work for you?' I said, confused.

'It's possible that the pages of the book will only appear for someone from your bloodline. The book was in your family library so it kind of makes sense. I've heard of similar books to this, but they're very rare.' he looked really invested in this, so as much as I didn't want to cut myself with a knife, I also didn't want to wuss out and say no, besides, I was interested now to see if it would work. I picked up the knife, and in one quick movement before I could change my mind, I slid the blade over the tip of my middle finger and held it over the cover of the book allowing my blood to spill into the design of the tree of life. The air crackled as soon as my blood touched the cover, I could feel a change in the atmosphere of the air around me, the smell of the old book filled my nostrils and I instantly felt like this book belonged to me. I picked it up from Lucas' knee and opened it to the first page and I could see words begin to fill up the pages. 'Holy shit, it worked.' I said, shocked.

Lucas stood up behind me and looked over my shoulder at the book. 'I never actually expected that to work you know,' he said quietly in awe. I could feel his breath on the back of my neck. I moved quickly and sat down on the bed to take a better look and Lucas came and sat beside me. I flicked through the pages, they were cramped with drawings, diagrams and spells written in a cursive style of handwriting that you didn't see anymore. I turned back to the first page and read the first line written there, 'For our heir, for only they can wield the fifth power and save our line.'

'What does that even mean?' I wondered out loud.

'It means you're the heir.' Lucas said with a small smile.

'But surely that could mean anyone in my family. It's not necessarily me. And what even is the fifth power.' I asked.

'I've never heard of a fifth power. But the book says 'For our heir', not for our heirs so it can only be about you as your blood activated the book. I've heard about books like this before, but honestly I've no idea how it works. A spell can be cast so the book only opens for people in the same bloodline, but I can't understand how a spell can be cast to only open for one person who is born hundreds of years after the book is written, it just can't be done. Well I wouldn't have thought it could be done until now. The only way to test it is to see if it works for anyone else in your family. Why don't you ask your Granny, the book was in her library so she might know more about it.'

'Yeah, I'll do that. Tomorrow. Its super late, or early, whatever. We better get some sleep.' I said.

'That's probably a good idea.' Lucas replied while staring intensely at me and making no move to leave.

'Sooo? Are you going to go then?' I said bluntly.

Lucas burst out laughing, 'You don't hold back do you.'

'Its a bit of a problem I have.' I said grimacing.

'I like it.' he smiled, 'Good night then Ashton, or good morning.' he said walking to the door.

'Night.' I replied, walking to the bed and throwing myself down on it face first. I rolled over on my back and shuffled backwards on my hands to get under the covers.

'Do you always get into bed like that?' Lucas said chuckling.

'Jesus christ, I thought you'd left.' I said exasperated.

He looked embarassed, 'Sorry, I just wanted to ask if you'd thought anymore about meeting Gavin tomorrow?' he asked.

'I don't know yet, I was going to talk to my Mum about it first I think before deciding either way.' I said.

'That's probably a good idea. Anyway good night, sorry for scaring you. I hope you can get some sleep now.' he said, and left.

I finally settled down to sleep and this time I was so tired I think I passed out as soon as my head hit the pillow.

CHAPTER 5

I woke up the next day to the sunlight shining through my windows. I had no idea what time it was but I guessed it was late. I felt hungover, my head was pounding and I felt queasy and weak. I instantly regretted waking up and wanted to go back to sleep, I rolled over facing away from the windows so the light didn't annoy me. I lifted my phone from the bedside table. Shit! It was after one in the afternoon. I really better get up. I wanted to talk to my Mum about Gavin. I slowly sat up and wave of sickness washed over me again. Oh God, I better not be getting sick on top of everything else that's all I needed. I was sore from the fight last night.

I got up and got ready as quickly as I was able and made my way downstairs and straight to my favourite place - the kitchen. I could already smell something cooking. When I went into the kitchen everyone was already there, talking and eating. As soon as I walked in Lucas looked up at me with that intense stare he had. It was nearly as if he sensed me entering the room. I got that electric shock sensation again. I didn't like the effect he had on me. I liked to be in control. I quickly looked away and walked over and sat down next to Adam who had his head down talking intently with Fiona. 'Good morning. What are you both looking so serious about?' I asked.

'Oh hey, how are you feeling after last night? You look really pale are you ok? Do you want something to eat or drink? I can get you something.' Fiona motored on.

'I'm not sure what to respond to first,' I laughed. 'Though I am a little offended you basically said I look like shit, so lets start with that.' I joked.

'Oh no I didn't mean that, I'm sorry I didn't mean that, you look amazing, I just meant are you ok, you do look a little pale?'

'Its fine relax, I was just winding you up. I do feel a bit off, I was worried I'm getting sick or something.' I said.

At that point Granny came over and put a plate with a fry in front of me, with bacon sausages, a fried egg, soda bread, potato bread and beans. 'Good morning dear, that will be the hangover from using your magic, you aren't used to it, it's like a muscle that you never exercise, it will be sore until you strengthen it. Magic works the same way and with yours being so powerful, I imagine it's a great deal worse for you. The more you use it, the easier it should be, until you have no after effects. You need to eat up, you'll feel better trust me.'

'Thanks Granny, it looks amazing, but I still feel really queasy, I'm not sure I can eat.' I said sadly looking at my amazing fry.

'Here, I'll get you a cup of tea, that always settles the stomach. Drink that first and then try a little food and see how you go.' she smiled.

'Thanks.' She brought me over a cup of tea.

I was surprised how much better I felt after drinking the tea, so much so that I devoured my fry. When everyone had finished eating Granny asked to talk to me and Mum out in the sunroom.

I sat down on the soft grey leather arm chair in the sunroom. Mum and Granny sat on matching armchairs facing me.

Mum looked nervous. 'What's wrong?' I asked feeling a bit

panicked at what else could be wrong.

'Everything's fine Ashton. We just wanted to make sure you're alright and to find out what happened last night. We were all too tired and beat up to talk about it last night.' Granny said calmly.

'Ok, well when we got to Dunluce Castle we decided that Mia and I would go in first and create a distraction and the rest of the guys were to follow to try and free Sophia, but we were captured by necromancers pretty much straight away and they took us to Sophia, who wasn't kidnapped afterall but in cohorts with her necromancer boyfriend John. They wanted to take me to see someone, but then we broke free and then you guys showed up and the fight ended. Then when we were leaving a necromancer stopped us on the road to give me a message.' I replayed it all in my head as I spoke.

'What was the message?' Granny asked.

'He said that Gavin wanted me to know that he didn't give me up and that he wants to meet with me and that he would get a message to me with the time and place. Oh and he said that all necromancers aren't evil.' I snorted.

My Mum visibly shrivelled up when I mentioned the name Gavin. So I added, 'I take it that my guess was right, Gavin is my Dad.'

'Yes dear, Gavin Kelly is your Dad.' my Granny confirmed. 'You mustn't go and meet with him. He could be dangerous.'

'Look I understand why you would think that, but I think I need to make up my own mind about that. I need answers about all of this, and I'm not going to get them hiding here. I want to know what he wants from me. Also he kept his word all these years about not telling anyone about me, so that has to count for something.' I said.

'Ashton, you can't meet with him, what if something

happens.Necromancers can't be trusted.' my Mum woke up out of her daze and spoke.

'Neither can Druids apparently, as we've just been betrayed by one of our own. How about we come to a compromise, because I've pretty much made up my mind and I don't want to go behind your back. I will only agree to meet him in a public place and someone can come with me and stay nearby?'

'No Ashton,' my Mum said, but Granny interjected. 'You can't stop her Maureen, you have to let her make her own decision, and she's right, we have been betrayed by one of our own and who knows if there are more traitors among us, so she's not any more safe among us. If we accompany her, we can keep her safe.'

'Fine, but I'm not happy about this.' Mum said with a frown. I took a good look at her and realised how tightly she was wound.

'It will be ok Mum, we'll be careful. Besides that's only if we even hear from him again. He is supposed to get a message to me. Lets just see what happens before we worry about it. What I would like to know is, do you really think we have more traitors amongst us? I've only got here and I still haven't met everyone. How many people know about me? About my power and about my Dad being a necromancer?' I asked.

'There are 18 Druid families living nearby. They all know and have all kept your secret all these years. Sophia's and Mia's Mother Lizzie is David's daughter. David is beside himself about whats happened. He called their Mum Emily and filled her in on what happened and she has disowned Sophia. Druid's take betrayal very seriously.'

'But that's her daughter. Why is she being treated so harshly when Mum wasn't? Maybe the necromancers have misled her.' I said, not knowing why I was so annoyed on Sophia's behalf, even after she betrayed me.

'There is a big difference between Sophia and I,' my Mum said coldly, 'Sophia knew what she was doing, I didn't know that your Father was a necromancer until it was too late and I didn't get away scot-free, many of the other Druids mistrusted me, I lost friends and I lost respect amongst our Grove, despite separating myself from your Father as soon as I knew who he really was and being left to raise a child on my own, whilst being judged by everyone including my own family.' my Mums voice got louder and louder as she spoke.

'I didn't know,' I said softly.

'No, you don't know, you've no idea what it was like Ashton, to live with that shame every day of my life since then, I've suffered plenty for my mistakes. So don't tell me I wasn't treated harshly.' she fumed, quieter now.

'I just meant, it seems extreme that her own Mother would be so quick to disown her, I'm new to being a Druid, but to me family has always came first, because that's what you taught me. I couldn't imagine disowning a member of my own family without giving them a chance first.' I said.

'I'm sure her Mum has her reasons, ' Granny said. 'Anyway, you had asked how many people know about you, there are 18 Druid families nearby and they all know. We are like one big family and we trust eachother. At least we did, after what Sophia has done there can only naturally be suspicion amongst us. We shared your secret to help keep you safe and its worked for almost 25 years. Now it seems by bringing you back here, it has put you in harms way. But it couldn't wait any longer. Without the ceremony your power would continue to grow but it would be erratic and out of control and you would risk exposing yourself.'

'Great.' I said sarcastically. Then added, 'Oh I nearly forgot, last night Lucas and I were in the library and he found a book I had been looking at. It has a really old leather cover with the Tree of Life engraved into it and all the pages were empty, he thought it might be some sort of blood magic but it wouldn't work with his blood, but I tried it with mine and it worked. All the pages filled with writing and drawings and diagrams. But on the first page it said 'For our heir, for only they can wield the fifth power and save our line.' Lucas said I must be the heir otherwise the book wouldn't show itself for me, but I thought maybe it work for anyone in our bloodline, he said the only way to test it is to get someone else in our family to try it. Do you think you could try?' I looked at both Mum and Granny expectantly but both of them were looking at me in shock.

'Ashton, where is the book now?' Granny asked.

'It's still in my room, why?'

'Show us,' she said getting up. 'Lets go to your room for some privacy.' she added.

We all made our way upstairs to my room. I showed them the empty book, then I used the Sgian Dubh again to slice my index finger this time, just to add another cut to my list of injuries. Again as soon as my blood touched the cover, the atmosphere in the air changed, a feeling of calm washed over me. I opened the pages and flicked through them, showing the contents, then went back to the first page and showed them the line which I had told them about.'

Mum gasped and my Granny's eyes widened as she covered her mouth with her hand. 'What's wrong?' I asked, getting a little freaked out by their reactions.

It was Granny who spoke. 'Ashton that book has been in the library my entire life, I tried it as did my Mother before me, as did my siblings and as have my children, and it has never revealed itself to anyone but you.'

'Wow, but what does that mean?'

'It means you really are the heir.' Mum said softly in awe.

'The heir of what? A creepy old book?' I said incredulous.

'I don't know,' Granny said, 'there is a story, it was more of a legend, that my Granny used to tell me about the book, but I always thought she was just having fun with us kids, so no one really believed it was real. '

'What is the legend?' I asked, now desperate to know and also amused to find out I was still the odd one out no matter where I went, between having all four types of magic, a necromancer for a Father and now this, I was just destined to be weird.

'I can still hear my Grandmother telling me the story now, 'The necromancers, once good and peaceful people, are now corrupted by their need for power. Not content with their diminished abilities they will stop at nothing to regain that power. With newfound secrets they will rise in power once again with one goal, to destroy the druids. Many will die if their plans come to pass. There will come a time when an heir is born, who this book was made for. Only the heir will have the power to open the book and stop them. Without the heir, all will be lost." Granny reminisced.

'This can't be real.' I whispered, 'I've only just found out I'm a Druid, why does it have to be me instead of someone who knows what they're actually doing. I'm going to chose to believe that this is just a story until proven otherwise.'

'In the mean time, read the book and see what you can learn from it.'

'Ok, I'll at least read it. If I can make sense of it.' I said reluctantly.

'Ashton, its probably best you don't tell anyone else about this, we don't know who we can trust at the moment.' Mum said.

THE DRUIDS OF BUSHMILLS - BOOK 1 - THE AWAKENING

'Your're probably right, but what about Lucas, he already knows.'

'Then you best talk to him and ask him not to let anyone else know about the book. It will also be a test to see if Lucas can be trusted.' she said.

'Ok I'll go and find him now.' I said.

We all left my room and went back down to the kitchen, it was then I realised that everywhere had been cleaned up from last night, there was no sign of what had happened here. I asked Granny, 'Who cleaned all this up?'

'Everyone helped this morning before you got up.' she replied.

'Oh now I feel awful for not helping.'

'Don't worry dear, I knew you would be exhausted after using your magic again, it didn't take us long at all.'

I knew where Lucas was as soon as I entered the room, it was like I could sense his presence without even looking, which was annoying. I walked over to him as he sat at the head of the dining table chatting to David, 'Hey Lucas, can I have a word?' Then added, 'Hows the head today David?'

I could feel Lucas staring at me just as I could feel my face getting hot. Thankfully David responded, 'Awk I'm fine, don't worry about me, I've had worse. How are you feeling? I'm sorry about Sophia, I feel responsible for her not only as High Priest of the Grove, but also as her Granda, I just can't believe she has done this.'

'You're not responsible for anyone but yourself David, no need to apologise. I can't help but feel a bit worried for Sophia, leaving her with the necromancers. She made a mistake but I don't feel right about it.' I said.

'You're very generous, but Sophia has made her choice.' David said firmly.

'But what if she made a bad choice and has now realised it's the wrong one. I have the least experience with necromancers, but from what I've been told they are ruthless, does she deserve to be left to her fate with them?'

'You have a unique way of thinking Ashton. I will think about what you have said.'

'Yeah unique that's me,' I mumbled under my breath. I smiled at David and turned to Lucas and pointed to the double doors leading to the sun room. He nodded and followed me.

'Hey whats up?' Lucas said once I closed the doors. When I turned around he was standing closer than I was comfortable with. Mainly because of the affect he was having on me. I inhaled a quick breath and spoke 'I just wanted to check if you had told anyone about last night with the book?'

'No, I haven't told a soul.'

I breathed a sigh of relief, 'Great well if you could just keep it that way for now, I think it's best to keep this to ourselves. With Sophia betraying us like that I'm not sure who can be trusted.' I said.

'How do you know you can trust me?'Lucas said.

'I don't, so prove to me that I can.'

'Fair enough. So what are you going to do with the book?'he said.

'I'm going to read it when I get a chance. I've only been here for a few days though and I'm already getting the feeling that getting the time might be difficult. It's been non stop drama.'

He laughed, 'Only since you got here.'

'Great so its my fault.'

'Pretty much, trouble seems to follow you around.' he teased.

'I've lead a boring, trouble free life until I moved here I'll have you know.'

'Yeah I believe you. So what are your plans for today?'

'Adam was supposed to be taking me out to show me the sights. I'm not sure if that's still happening though after last night.'

'Would you mind if I joined you?' he asked, I could see red creeping into his neck and face, under his golden tan.

'No, well as long as Adam doesn't mind, I don't mind. Lets go ask him.'

We went back into the kitchen, Adam and FIona were where I had left them earlier. 'Hey Adam are you still up for going out today? Lucas was going to come too if that's alright, why don"t you come too Fiona?'

'Yeah I'm up for it.' Fiona said enthusiastically.

'Yeah sure, the more the merrier.' Adam said and I couldn't help but notice the hint of sarcasm in his voice. 'I'll need to go home and get my car though then I can come back and pick you guys up? My Mum has already left and she was my lift.'

'Why don't we borrow one of Granny's cars? She told me I could.'

'Yeah that will work.' Adam said.

I turned to where Granny was now making tea at the worktop. 'Granny would it be alright if I borrowed a car? We were going to go out.' I asked.

'Yes go ahead dear, the keys are in the key box in the garage, you can take whatever car you want, but I thought you'd like the range rover.'

'Thanks Granny.' I said giving her a quick hug.

I turned back to Adam, Fiona and Lucas who was staring yet again. 'Good to go, where did you guys get the clean clothes from?'
'Oh your Granny brought me up clean clothes this morning,' Fiona said gesturing at her clothes, she was wearing pink strappy sandals, light wash skinny jeans and blue cami top with an oversized white cardigan. She looked as glamourous as she did last night.

'You look great.' I said. She smiled back at me.

'Yeah your Granny seems to be prepared for everything, she gave us some of your Uncle Malcolms clothes, not my style but I think I make it work.' Adam said.

'Ok happy days, lets go.'

CHAPTER 6

We went through the kitchen and utility room to the garage. There were 6 cars parked. I instantly seen and fell in love with the electric blue range rover. I opened the key box and found the key. I opened it got in the drivers side and Fiona got in the passenger seat, the two boys got in the back. The car was kitted out with soft black leather heated seats. It was nearly as nice on the inside as it was on the outside. When everyone was in I used the fob to open the garage door. 'So where to?' I asked.

'Let's go to the Billberry Mill for a coffee.' Fiona said.

'Ok sounds good, but you will have to direct me.'

I drove whilst we chatted, all the while looking at the gorgeous surroundings, green hills and fields with cows and sheep scattered throughout them grazing on grass and you could see the ocean from the road. I really loved this place.

It turned out Billberry Mill was in the centre of Bushmills village. It was a short drive only around 5 minutes away. There were lots of other shops nearby including a tourist gift shop, an Antique shop, grocery stores, a butchers, a Fruit shop that was also a florists, a wool shop, some clothing and shoe shops and a book shop that I was definitely going to explore later. There was plenty packed into this little village with a mixture of old and modern buildings and an old clock tower overlooking it all. I was going to enjoy exploring it.

When we parked we went into Billberry Mill and sat on the cosy brown leather sofas and Lucas went and ordered us all a coffee and a delicious caramel square. 'So where to next.' I asked.

'Where ever you like. There's Portballintrae, another village nearby with a nice beach, or Portrush with lots of fun fair rides and another beach which is good for surfing or we could go to Bushmills Distillery for a tour and some whiskey or the Giants Causeway.'

'I've heard of the Giant's Causeway before, what is it?' I asked.

Fiona groaned, 'I can tell you that it's not somewhere I want to walk in these sandals.'

'That's ok,' I laughed, 'We can go somewhere else, I don't mind. I kind of want to look in the book store anyway.'

'The Giant's Causeway is amazing, it's a long ass walk but it's worth it. It's set on a cliff and is made up of columns of rocks that look like steps. That's why it's known as the Giant's Causeway as it looks like steps made for a Giant, or by a Giant. It's told by tour guides and locals that it was formed by volcanic activity millions of years ago, but although the cliffside has been there for millions of years, the unique shape was actually formed by Druids, during a battle just over a thousand years ago. The story as Druid's know it is different. Branwen the High Priestess at the time found an ancient sacred crystal known as the Nexium. The Nexium had been sought after for many years as it was said to possess the ability to harness and amplify the energies of the land. It was also known for its healing properties. Branwen believed that the Nexium should be kept secret and hidden, so it couldn't be used by darker forces who wanted to exploit its power, she feared that in the wrong hands it could be used to amplify dark magic, unleashing chaos and suffering.

Elara was Branwen's friend, however she believed what she was doing was wrong and that the Nexium's potential should be explored and its energies harnessed to heal and bring prosperity to their people and even ward off dark forces.They clashed in a bitter battle. The Giant's Causeway was already a great source of natural power, but as their battle wore on and they both became tired and their ancestors refused to help them, Branwen drained energy from the volcanic rock on the cliff, partially destroying it, leaving it as it now stands. Upon realising what she had done, she relinquished the fight, and gave the Nexium to Elara who became the new High Priestess. Elara used the Nexium to heal and restore the land however the appearance remained the same. She then hid the Nexium. It has never been seen again.'

I was stunned by Adam's story, that was batshit crazy. 'Wow, that can't be true. Is it true?'

He laughed, 'Well that's the story that's been passed down through the centuries.'

'I definitely need to go and see this place. Can we go tomorrow?'

'Sure,' he said, 'but don't forget that your ceremony is tomorrow evening.'

'Oh yeah, that's right. About that, have any of you had your ceremony yet? I've got no idea what to expect, no one has told me, not that there has been much time with everything that's been going on from I got here.'

'Lucas and I have.' Fiona said, then she added. I looked at her confused, wondering how she knew Lucas had as well. When she seen the confused look on my face she burst out laughing. 'I suppose you wouldn't know. Lucas and I are twins.'

'You're joking. I didn't even know you were related, never mind twins. Now that you mention it, I can see the resemblance. How did I miss this?' I said.

Lucas and Fiona both laughed at exactly the same time and made exactly the same sound. 'Oh my God, that was creepy, you even laugh the same.'

We all erupted in laughter.

When we had all calmed down, Lucas spoke. 'We had our ceremony 6 months ago. Ours was a little different as we are twins, so our ceremony was a joint ceremony. I don't want to spoil it for you, but it involves preparing offerings for your Druid Ancestors and then you make your vows and your ancestors will give a sign that they have heard you. It can be kind of intense. Then afterwards there will be a party.'

'That doesn't sound too bad,' I mused, 'especially the after party.'

Fiona chuckled, 'I knew I liked you. So where to next then?'

'How about we go to the book shop and then to Portrush? I think I was there once when I was little.'

'Sounds good.' Adam replied.

We finished up and left and walked down the street to a little bookshop called Causeway Books. Inside was full of floor to ceiling bookcases filled with a wide range of used and new books with glass display stands set about the place with retro toys and games inside. This was right up my street. The owner looked up at us from the book that he was reading and smiled when we entered. 'Hi, how are ya's? Are you looking for anything specific?'.

'Hi, no not looking for anything in particular, I just wanted to have a look around.' I said.

'No problem, just let me know if you need anything.' he said, smiling warmly at me, his gaze lingered for a second and then went back to reading his own book.

Fiona and I browsed the books and I picked up a few that I wanted to buy. Adam and Lucas were looking at the retro games consoles in the glass cabinets, arguing over whether the SNES was better than the N64. I went to the till to pay. The owner looked at me and smiled again, 'So you like reading then?' he said, taking the small stack of books from me.

'Erm yeah, that's why I came into a book shop.' I replied.

Adam and Lucas burst out laughing. I got really embarassed at my bluntness and could feel my face go purple. 'I didn't mean to be rude, I just meant that's why I came in, I'm new to town and was so happy to see a book shop, so wanted to come in for a look. I like to read when I get the time.' I let out a breath.

The man laughed, 'It's ok, it was a silly question. Just not many young ones these days like to read.' He gave me another warm smile. He looked to be in his mid forties with greying brown hair and green eyes. I felt like I recognised him from somewhere. I realised he was staring, 'So uh, how much do I owe you?' I asked.

'Oh don't worry about it, no charge.' he said.

'What? No, I can't do that, please how much is it?' I said getting embarassed now.

'Honestly, I'm just glad to see you reading.' he replied.

'I would really feel better about it if I paid you.' This was getting weird.

'Please, it's on me. Just come back again. You can pay me for the next lot of books.' he said kindly.

Absolutely mortified, I mumbled my thanks and went to leave when Lucas said sarcastically, 'Does that mean I don't have to pay for that SNES, or is that rule just reserved for beautiful young girls, you creep.'

'Oh my God Lucas, don't be so rude, I'm so sorry, we're leaving.' I said my face now scarlet.

'He has a point.' Adam said.

'That's ok, it's nice to see that you have these young men looking out for you. I'm more than happy for you boys and lady,' he said nodding at Fiona, 'to pick a book free of charge. You can read can't you.' he said winking at me. I snorted out a laugh, Fiona giggled and Adam laughed too, Lucas retorted, 'Yes I can read, I just don't fancy any of the fusty old books in your shop.' and promptly stormed out.

'I'm sorry,' I said, 'I don't know what's got into him. Thanks for the books, I'm sure I'll be back again soon.'

When we were back outside the shop, I rounded on Lucas, 'What the hell was that?'

'That guy was being a creep.' he said furiously.

'Oh come on, he was just being nice. I admit it was a bit weird but I think he was genuine.'

'Don't be so naive Ashton.'

'You don't even know me Lucas.' I replied scathingly.

'Fine, whatever.' he huffed and stomped off down the street. Fiona looked at me apologetically and went after him.

Adam fell into step beside me, 'Well that was interesting.' he said humorously.

I laughed, 'Yeah that's a word for it. What's his problem?'

'I get the impression he likes you, though he's taking the overprotectiveness a bit far. I don't like it, you're my friend and he's not allowed to play with you.'

I laughed again, 'Now who's being overprotective. Do you really think he likes me?'

'He called you beautiful.' Lucas replied dryly.

'I thought he was just speaking in general.' I said.

'You really are naive.' He said jokingly, so of course I elbowed him.

When we got back to the car, Lucas and Fiona were waiting for us. I unlocked the car and Adam and Fiona got in. Lucas fixed me with that intense stare he has. 'I'm sorry, I was out of order, I just thought that guy was being an old creep. I overreacted.'

'You're right you did. But whatever, just don't do it again. I can defend myself you know.' I said.

'I don't doubt that, I really am sorry Ashton. Don't let it spoil the rest of the day, I promise I'll behave.'

'Ok, well let's go.' I walked round to my side of the car and got in.

'I started the car and made the short 15 minute journey to Portrush.'

We went to Curry's, an amusement park that was apparently famous. I went on The Cyclone with Fiona, all 4 of us went on The Big Dipper, Adam, Fiona and I went on The Turtle Splash and I got soaked because I was in the front, we paid for the photo of me grimacing whilst getting drenched, then we all went on the Carousel with the little kids which was hilarious and we went on the Dodgems and got told off multiple times for driving the wrong way so we could crash into eachother and then Lucas and I went on the Ghost Train. When we were done with the rides we played the machines and Lucas got 1000 tokens and used them to get me a small Squishmallow and a few sweets for Fiona and Adam.

'I am shattered after that, 1 seen milkshakes upfront, lets go get one then we can decide where to go for dinner.' I said.

'We definitely have to go to the chippy at the East Strand.' Adam said.

'Suits me.' I said.

We went and got milkshake and I couldn't resist some candy floss, never mind dinner.

We walked over to the chippy at the East Strand, which was luckily where I had parked my car anyway, and got a chippy, then sat and ate and watched all the surfers braving the cold at this time in the evening. I was just thinking that I couldn't remember the last time I'd had so much fun, despite all the craziness of the past few days, when my phone rang.

'Hi Mum, you ok?'I picked up.

'Ashton, a note has just been delivered for you. Someone knocked the door, but by the time your Uncle Malcolm answered it, there was no one there but the note was stuck to the door with your name on it. It must be from Gavin. Where are you?'

'I'm in Portrush, I think we were going to leave soon anyway, so I'll see you when I get back.'

'Ok, see you soon sweetheart. Be careful.'

'Bye Mum.'

When I hung up Lucas obviously reading the look on my face asked, 'What's wrong?'

'A note was just delivered to the house for me, my Mum thinks its from Gavin. Are you guys ready to head back? I'm tired anyway and I want to see what it says.'

'Lets go.' Adam said.

We all picked up our rubbish and put it in the bin and made our way to the car.

When we got in I spoke, 'I've just realised I don't know where any of you guys live.'

'You don't need to take me home, I want to make sure you get home safe, I live close enough to walk or if my Mum isn't already at your house I'm sure she won't mind coming to pick me up.'

'I think we should all stay together. We'll come too.' Lucas said.

'I'm touched, but there's really no need. I'll be fine. I'm safe in the car.' I said.

'I'd feel better about making sure you're home safe too,' Fiona said, 'It's you that the necromancers are after and a car isn't going to stop them. Well unless you run them over.' she added seriously. I laughed nervously, hoping she was joking.

'You all just want to see what the note says, don't you?' I joked.

'You got me, now lets get a move on, I bet your Granny has some good desserts.' Adam replied.

We made the quick journey home, chatting and joking about our day.

When we got there, I pulled up in the courtyard and got out. I'm sure Granny wouldn't mind me parking here, everyone else did, and it was more convenient than the garage.

I grabbed my books from the boot, but Lucas was there quick as a shot to take them off me and carry them in. 'Thanks, I could have done that myself,' I grumbled. When we went into the house, everyone was in the sitting room for once, sitting on comfortable chairs, looking serious.

'Hey, what's up?' I asked.

'Oh, I'm glad you're here, I was worried about you being out after getting this note.' Mum said.

'Can I see it?'

My mum handed me the small envelope with the tape still stuck to it obviously from where it had been stuck to the door. I opened it and unfolded the small piece of paper inside and read it out loud, 'Meet me tomorrow at 12 at The Billberry Mill and I will explain everything. Gavin'. I turned the paper over in my hand, 'Is that it? I was expecting something a bit more, how do I even know this is from him?'

'You don't,' my Mum said. 'I don't think you should go Ashton, it's too dangerous.'

'Look we've talked about this already, I'm going. It's a public place, nothing is going to happen.'

'I thought you'd say that, but I had to try. But you're not going alone.' she said.

'That's fine, I can live with that. I'm not sure I want to go on my own anyway.'

'I will come with you.' Mum said.

'Mum, I'm not sure you should go, not with your history, maybe someone else could come with me.'

'I'll go.' Lucas and Adam said simultaneously.

'There we go, sorted, the 3 of us can go.' I said.

'Well you can't leave me out.' Fiona added. I smiled at her.

'Great, I'll pick you guys up at around 11.30 tomorrow. Oh I still don't know where any of you live.' I remembered outloud.

'Why don't you all stay here again, then I can make you a good breakfast in the morning before you go.' Granny said speaking for the first time since we came in. Then added, 'I can send you all up more clean clothes to your rooms.'

'Only if that's ok with you.' Lucas said.

'Of course, you're all always welcome here. Have you had anything to eat yet? I can make something if you like.'

'We've had dinner, but I won't say no to dessert if you have any.' Adam said patting his belly with a grin.

Granny laughed, 'Of course, I always keep extra to hand in case you come around Adam. What about the rest of you?'

'I'm good Granny, I'm stuffed, I might go and get a bath, I'm beat after today.'

'Yeah I think I'll join you.' Fiona said.

'Oh maybe I'll pass on dessert and join the girls then.' Adam joked.

'Behave yourself Adam, you're not to old for a clip round the ear,' Granny scolded him and we all laughed.

Fiona and I made our way upstairs and parted ways at the top to go to our rooms. I was looking forward to getting a bath and relaxing. I went into my room and ran a bath. I just had the bath as full as I could get it without it overflowing once I got in and was turning off the taps, when there was a knock at my door. Come in I called from the en suite. When I turned the taps off I got up and turned and Lucas was there, setting my books down on one of my beside cabinets.

'Hi, I forgot to give you your books back. I didn't mean to disturb you.' he said quietly.

'That's ok I forgot too, thanks for bringing them up. Did you not stay for dessert?'

'No, I had enough at dinner. I think I'll get an early night too. It's been a busy few days.' he said.

'That's putting it mildly,' I said dryly and he laughed.

'Are you nervous about tomorrow?' he asked.

'Honestly, I haven't even really had time to think about it. I've never known anything about my Dad until now, but I never felt like I was missing anything either, but now that I have the opportunity to meet him, even though I know he's supposed to be bad, I guess I'm a bit excited. Is that weird?'

'No, well maybe it's a bit weird. But I think I get it. Fiona and I never got to meet our Father, he died before we were born, so I can understand to some extent.'

'That's awful, I didn't know, I'm sorry.' I said walking over to sit down on my bed.
'It's ok, you can't miss what you never knew.' he said as he came to sit beside me.

'That's a lie and you know it.' I blurted out. He laughed, 'Yeah I guess you're right. My Mum doesn't talk about him ever, but I was always sort of curious. It never seemed to bother Fiona the way it bothered me. I used to pester my Mum with questions about my Dad, but she always brushed my questions off. It must be too difficult for her to talk about.'

'That's so sad, your poor Mum.'

He looked up at me, I just now realised our close proximity, somehow we had turned side ways to face eachother, knees touching, we were openly staring at eachother, I should have been getting embarassed right about now, but I didn't care and couldn't stop looking at the way his hair had fell across his forehead and I had to resist the urge to push it back. Suddenly as if struck by lightening, he surged forward placing both his hands around my wrists and I thought he was going to kiss me and in that moment I wanted nothing else, but he stopped just short, and gave me the softest kiss on the corner of my mouth, sending an electric shock sensation throughout my entire body, I released a breath I didn't even realise I was holding. Then he was up on his feet walking towards the door and called back without even looking, 'Goodnight Ashton, I'll see you in the morning.'

I sat there absolutely dumbstruck. Annoyed by my reaction to him, and that I wanted him to kiss me so badly and frustrated that it had ended so abruptly. Maybe he changed his mind. I didn't know what to make of Lucas, I mean he was gorgeous, of that there was no doubt, but he was also really intense and was weirdly overprotective even though we had just met and I wasn't sure if I loved that or hated it.

I got a bath and got into bed and decided to read 'my' book to put Lucas out of mind. I used the Sgian Dubh to cut my thumb this time. Once again as soon as my blood touched the Tree of Life on the cover of the book, the atmosphere in the air changed, and I got the strange sense that this book belonged to me. Even though I had physically used my abilities, the sensation I got when I opened this book told me this was all real, that magic and Druid's and this life that was now mine was real.

I opened the front cover and re-read the first line. 'For our heir, for only they can wield the fifth power and save our line.' What could the fifth power be, I wondered.

I turned the page. It read

In the sacred twilight, on the eve of a Druid's twenty-fifth year,
They shall embark upon a solemn rite.
With heart full of gratitude,
they shall assemble offerings of nature's bounty,
Through the whispers of wind and the echoes of time,

the spirits of our ancestors shall infuse them with their power.
Thus completing their transformation, A Druid's new beginning.

That was obviously about the ceremony.

The heir of our bloodline shall have the gift times five
Earth, Air, Water, Fire and Spirit.
Should they follow the path we set forth for them,
Our ancestors will bestow them with the coveted fifth power
Thus our line will endure

So the fifth power is spirit. Whatever that means. I will ask Granny and Mum tomorrow. I leafed my way through more of the pages but I could barely keep my eyes open, the last few days finally caught up with me and I drifted off for a much needed sleep.

CHAPTER 7

I woke up to someone calling my name. It sounded like they were calling from really far away, I couldn't quite make out who it was, but they were definitely calling my name. I tried to open my eyes but they were so heavy, so I decided it mustn't be important and began to drift off, when I heard the voice again, urgent now and more persistent. 'Ashton, you must wake up. You must listen. You are in grave danger. You must hide the book. They are coming for it and you.'

I jerked up right in bed, fully alert now and looked around in the darkness to see where the voice came from. It was useless as it was pitch black and my eyes hadn't adjusted yet to the darkness. 'Who's there?' I said and could hear the tremble in my own voice.

'It doesn't matter who I am, you must listen. Hide the book.'

'Yeah sure, I'm going to listen to some weird voice I heard in the dark.' I turned on the lamp on the bedside cabinet, but there was no one there. I wondered had I imagined the whole thing and I was annoyed at having been woke up. I took one last glance around the room and switched the lamp off again and went back to sleep.

CHAPTER 8

I woke up feeling refreshed the next morning. I felt nervous about seeing Lucas after last night, but I decided to put our almost kiss and his swift exit to the back of my mind. I got ready and went downstairs to the kitchen. It seemed I was the last one there as usual. 'Morning everyone.' I called out. Instantly noticing Lucas at the top of the table with Fiona and Adam.

'You look like you got a good sleep dear,' Granny said distracting me from replaying last night over in my head again.

'I did, I feel good. Did you sleep ok?' I asked, looking at my Granny and realising she looked a little tired and the past few days were probably catching up with her too. She spent so much time looking after everyone else, who looked after her.

'Yes dear I'm fine, don't worry about me.' Granny said unsurprisingly. She would never admit to being less than one hundred percent.

'Why don't you let me cook breakfast Granny? I'm getting out of practice, I haven't cooked a thing from I've got here.'

'Oh you know I like cooking, I don't mind.' she replied.

'Well so do I, and you said this is my home now too, so you're going to have to get used to me liking to cook sometimes too, now go and sit down and do what you're told.'

Granny chuckled as she went to sit down and I went about making everyone breakfast. It felt good to do something for Granny for once. After I'd finished serving everyone else I sat down to my own breakfast of omlette.

'This isn't half bad.' Adam said through a mouthful. 'I give it a 9 out of 10.'

'Oh really, and what can you cook?' I asked.

'I know my way around a microwave.' he retorted and we all laughed.

'So how are you feeling about meeting Gavin this morning.' Fiona asked.

'Awk I'm ok, I'm not worried, I'm just more intrigued about what he has to say.'

'We're leaving,' my Mum interjected.

I looked at her puzzled, 'Where are you going?'

'I know you don't think I should come, but your Granny, Uncle Malcolm, David, Leona and I are going to go on ahead of you guys just to make sure it's not a trap and that there are no other necromancers around, we just want to keep you safe and we're going to do that from a distance. I want one of you to go into the Billberry with Ashton and the other two to wait outside.' My mum said looking at Adam, Lucas and Fiona.

'Is that really necessary in broad daylight?'

'We're just taking precautions. I promise we will keep our distance and only come if necessary.'

'Ok, well I guess we will see you soon.'

We got ready and left in my Range Rover at around 11.30. The closer it got to meeting him the more nervous I got. Adam had run out to the car first so he could get in the passenger side, leaving Fiona and Lucas in the back. 'You ok there Ashton? Your fingers are going to drum a hole in the steering wheel if you keep that up.' Adam said.

'I didn't even realise I was doing it, I guess I'm a little nervous.'

'It'll be fine, don't worry. We will all be there. Just go and hear him out.'

'That's what I'm worried about, what he has to say. Not what he is going to do.'

'Well we're all here for you.' Adam said uncharacteristically serious.

'Thanks Adam.' I glanced up and looked in the rear view mirror and Lucas was staring back at me.

When we arrived, I parked and we decided that Fiona would go in with me and the boys would wait outside. We couldn't' see anyone else that had arrived early, but I got a text from my Mum saying it looked all clear. We got to the Billberry 10 minutes early, so Fiona and I went in and ordered for us and the boys and took them a coffee to go outside. I protested when I realised they were planning on standing at the door like two bouncers. It would be enough to put anyone off so I got them to move a little up the street so that they could still see in the window but didn't look so suspicious. Fiona and I sat down on the comfy brown leather sofas we had sat on the day before and waited. I looked at my watch and it was exactly one minute to twelve. I was practically bouncing in my seat, my leg was jittering, my foot tapping.

'Hey, calm down, people will think you're on drugs or something.' Fiona joked.

'I know, I know, I just wasn't expecting to be this nervous. I need a distraction. Talk to me.'

'Ok how about this? I think my brother fancies you.' Fiona said amused. My face went the colour of beetroot. 'I'm guessing by your reaction, you like him too.'

'Lets talk about something else.' I said hurriedly. 'It has to be weird me talking to you about your brother.' She laughed again.

'I don't want any of the details, I can just tell he likes you, what's not to like. I just thought I'd suss out if Adam's competition for him.'

'Adam?' I said confused, 'why would Adam be competition? Oh no it's not like that with me and Adam, he's just a joker. He flirts with everyone, he doesn't mean anything by it.'

'OH-MY-GOD, you are so blind.' She laughed again.

'I really think you've got it wrong, Adam doesn't like me like that.'

'If you say so.' she said dryly.

'So, are you seeing anybody? I said changing the subject and the focus from me.

'No, not really, I go on dates, but most of the guys we socialise with I've known since we were kids and I've seen picking their noses or crying for their Mummys, its kind of unappealing.'

I burst out laughing at that. 'Yeah I get your point.'

It was ten past twelve now with still no sign of Gavin. I sent Adam a text, 'See anything yet?'

'Nope, no one even looking this direction.' he replied.

'Where is he?' I said to Fiona, 'Maybe he came and seen that I wasn't alone and left again.' I said doubtfully.

'I don't think it's a good idea to leave you alone.' she said.

'Maybe you could just sit over there at that empty table by the window?' I asked.

She reluctantly got up and moved to the other table.

I was obsessively checking my phone. I sent my Mum a text. 'Any sign of him yet?'

'No not yet sweetheart.' she replied.

I waited and waited, but when it got to twelve forty five I faced reality, he wasn't coming.

I got up and Fiona fell into step beside me. 'Lets go, he's not coming.' I felt completely deflated. I had got myself all hyped up for this only to be disappointed.

We met up with the guys outside. 'Sorry Ashton, something maybe came up.' Adam said.

I was embarassed and felt like crying. I didn't think it would affect me so badly if he didn't show up and I was mortified I had an audience to my Dad standing me up. I sent my Mum a text to say we were leaving. She replied immediately to say they were leaving too.

CHAPTER 9

When we arrived back to Granny's house I pulled up in the courtyard behind my Uncle Malcolm's car and it was clear something was wrong. Uncle Malcolm looked furious.

'Hey, what's wrong?' I asked getting out of my car.

'Someone's been in the house. We should have seen this coming. The Necromancer's were only trying to get us out of the house because they wanted in.' Uncle Malcolm ranted.

'But why, what could they want us out of the house for?' I asked.

'I don't know but it can't be good.' he replied.

Then it struck me, the book and the weird dream I'd had the night before. I sprinted into the house and run up the stairs to my bedroom and looked on the bedside cabinet where I'd left the book. It was gone.

'What is it? What's wrong?' It was Lucas who had got there first.

'The book, it's gone.' I said.

Uncle Malcolm, Granny and my Mum appeared at the doorway, with Adam and Fiona following not far behind.

'What's happened,' Granny said.

Remembering that only Mum, Granny, Lucas and I knew about the book, I replied, 'I just wanted to make sure none of my stuff had been stolen.'

Adam looked at me as if I was insane, 'Seriously Ashton, Necromancers break in and you think they'd be interested in the contents of your underwear drawer.' he laughed.
'Hey, I have some nice stuff.' I said feeling stupid.

Granny gave me a strange look and I nodded at her.

'Ok, let's go and take a look and see if they have taken or disturbed anything else. Adam, Fiona, can you check around the stone circle and the Blackthorn tree and the outhouses, maybe the necromancers were trying to disrupt Ashton's ceremony tonight. Malcolm and Leona, you check the grounds to the front and the sides of the house, you know that area best. David can you check the rest of this floor with Lucas. Ashton, Maureen and I will check downstairs.'

Granny, Mum and I went downstairs and into the games room and closed the door so no one could hear us. 'Tell us.' Mum barked.

'It's the book, it's gone.' I said.

Mum gasped.

'But I don't understand, why would anyone take the book, when only I can open it? It doesn't make sense. Also I had a dream last night and I'm now wondering if it was a dream at all. I could hear a voice calling my name, and it said to hide the book, they're coming for it. But when I turned the light on there was no one there. I must have fell back to sleep so I assumed it was a dream, but what if it wasn't?'

'Tell us exactly what happened.' Granny commanded.

'I heard a voice calling my name, but they sounded really far away, then they got louder and they told me I had to wake up and hide the book because *'they're coming for it and you'* and something about being in grave danger. Honestly the whole thing felt like a dream. I asked who it was and they said it didn't matter. I couldn't see because it was dark, so I turned the light on and there was no one there and I didn't hear the voice again. That was it.'

'I don't know whose the voice was that spoke, but they've answered your question about why they have taken the book because they can't open it without you. They don't plan on opening it without you, they are just going to come back for you later. It was easier to get us out of the house first to steal the book. So the most important question now is, how did they know about the book. Did you tell anyone else about the book Ashton?'

'No, just both of you and Lucas, because he was with me when I first opened the book. I asked him not to tell anyone about the book yesterday before we went out and he said he wouldn't, but then how else would they know.'

'Lets not jump to conclusions until we have all the facts.' Granny said.

'None of this makes sense. It was 2 days ago or nights ago, that Gavin gave me the message about meeting him. How could Lucas have possibly known then that I could open the book. But then I found him in the library with the book on that same night. Maybe he was going to try and steal the book then, only I found him with it in the library and stopped him. Is it possible that someone else could open the book?'

'Yes, it's possible, though unlikely that after hundreds of years that there are two heirs in one generation.' Granny said.

'What will we do about Lucas? I told him to prove to me that he could be trusted and not twenty four hours later the book has been stolen.'

'We don't do anything, we need proof first and at the moment I am struggling to come up with any sort of motivation that Lucas could have for stealing the book or helping the necromancers steal the book.'

'Lets get him in here and ask him outright, surely his reaction should help us figure out if he had anything to do with it.'

'I don't know if that's a good idea Ashton, it will let him know we're on to him if it was him.' Mum said.

'He will know we are on to him anyway, as he knows he was the only other person who knew about the book other than us. I can't talk to him and pretend everything is normal when I'm suspicious of him.'

'I don't think it's a bad idea.' Granny said.

'I'll go upstairs and find him.' I left the games room and got half way upstairs when Lucas started coming down.

'Hey Lucas, I was just coming to find you, Granny wants you in the games room.' I said, a hard tone to my voice. Lucas just looked at me blankly. David appeared behind him, eyebrow raised. 'Everything ok Ashton?' he asked.

'Yeah all good, we didn't find anything missing, although we haven't finished looking. What about you?'

'Nothing seems amiss, it's a strange one for sure. Unless they came to mess with your ceremony, I'm not sure what they came for. I'm going to go check out back with Adam and Fiona.

'So your Granny suspects me.' Lucas stated.

'Wouldn't you?' I asked.

He didn't respond. We went into the games room where Mum

and Granny were waiting.

'Lucas, I'm sure you are aware, you are the only one that knew about the book other than Maureen, Ashton and I. Ashton asked you to keep its existance and that she is heir a secret and now someone has broken into our home and stolen it.' Granny said without preamble. 'Did you have something to do with this Lucas?'

'I understand why you might think that, but no I didn't have anything to do with it going missing. I wouldn't betray Ashton like that. Not only that, I knew I was the only other person who knew about the book so all suspicion would fall on me if anything happened to it.' he replied evenly.

If he was lying he was damn good at it.

'That makes sense.' Granny said.

'Correct me if I'm wrong, but the book itself wasn't a secret before now. What if there is another heir? And the necromancers aren't aware that Ashton can open it. The timing is suspicious with the recent discovery that Ashton's blood can open the book, but it could just be a coincidence.'

'You're right that the book wasn't a secret. I will have to think about this.' Granny said. 'In the mean time, Ashton you need to start getting ready for your ceremony tonight. It will start at around 10.30pm when darkness falls. Go with your Mum and she will help you with what you need. I'll catch up with you both later.'

We left Lucas with Granny, I couldn't help but look back as I left the room and my eyes met his, he smiled as if to say he was ok.

'Lets go get some lunch before we start preparing for your ceremony.' Mum said interrupting my thoughts.

CHAPTER 10

After lunch, Mum took me out to the clearing past the outhouses. Everyone else filled us in that nothing else seemed to be missing or even touched. If the wards hadn't of been disturbed we would never have known that anyone was here, other than the book being missing and even then I might have thought I had misplaced it.

'Mum, I've been meaning to ask, how is Mia?'

'She's holding up, she's angry with her sister but she doesn't want to leave her in the necromancer's hands.'

'I can't say I blame her. I get it, she made a mistake, but does she really deserve to be left to her fate with the necromancers?' I asked.

'What she did was unforgiveable Ashton, you could have been killed. Who knows what the necromancers wanted you for.'

'You're only saying that because I'm your daughter, imagine if Sophia was your daughter. Would you just leave her there?' I said angrily.

My mum was silent for a moment and I thought she wasn't going to answer me and then she said, 'I guess you're right, I wouldn't.'

'Then I think we should try and help her. After my ceremony. At the moment it seems like we are just reacting to whatever the necromancers do next. We need to be smart and make a plan and maybe we will get the book back in the process.'

'You're getting ahead of yourself Ashton, lets focus on your ceremony first. Besides, only David can make a decision on what to do about Sophia.'

'Why because he's her Granda?'

'No, because he's the High Priest. He's pretty easy going, but he is still the leader of our Grove.'

'Ok, well I will ask him after the ceremony.' I said.

My Mum raised her eyes to the skies, clearly exasperated with me.

'Ok, so back to your ceremony. You need offerings to give to our ancestors. It has to be things that you have grown or picked yourself, it can't be store bought. We have plenty around here that we can use.'

We went into the outhouse and grabbed a couple of bowls and a kneeling cushion each and walked past the clearing to the fields beyond. There was a little allotment to the left just in front of the fields.
We filled our bowls with strawberries, raspberries and gooseberries and I picked up a few apples that had fallen from the apple tree. We took them back to the house and washed them.

When we had finished we put them in the fridge for later. Mum took me upstairs to her room to show me something. 'I had this made specially for your ceremony.' Mum said walking into her wardrobe and bringing out a gorgeous silver velvet robe, the inside was the deepest royal blue and it was finished with with blue trim. On the silver was an intricate symbol sewn into the velvet. I touched the symbol, 'What is this?' I asked.

'It's a triskele, it reminds us of the connection between our ancestors, our past, present and future.'

'I love it, thank you.' I said.

'I would like to say I made it myself, like your Granny made mine, but I don't have her skills in the sewing department, Leona made it for you.' she said.

'I will thank her when I see her. Who's going to be at the ceremony tonight?' I asked.

'All the family - Granny, me, Uncle Malcolm, Uncle Mark, Aunt Emma and your cousins Anna, Jacob and Caitlyn are coming, they should be here soon. And then there will be at least one representative from the other 18 Druid families nearby including Leona and your friends, Fiona, Lucas and Adam. Oh and David too, he's never too far from your Granny.'

'What's that mean?' I asked, oblivious.

'Oh, I just think Granny and David are awfully friendly.' she said with a grin.

'No way! I'd no idea, though now that you say it, it kind of makes sense. He has been around a lot from we've got here. Do you think they don't want people to know they're a couple?'

'Oh, I don't even think they know they're a couple. Not yet, anyway.' she laughed and I joined in. I liked the idea of Granny having someone to look out for her.

'Oh Mum, I meant to ask, what is spirit?'

My Mum jerked her head up. 'What do you mean?'

'Well I was reading the book last night before I went to sleep and it mentioned that the heir would have the gift of spirit. Is that the fifth power?'

'What exactly did it say Ashton?' my Mum asked hyper alert now.

'I can't remember exactly, I think it was

The heir of our bloodline shall have the gift times five
Earth, Air, Water, Fire and Spirit.
Should they follow the path we set forth for them,
Our ancestors will bestow them with the coveted fifth power
Thus our line will endure'

'Do you know what that means?' I asked

'Necromancers power is called spirit. It's not associated with Druids usually' my Mum said quietly.

'But what exactly is spirit?'

'It's the ability to see and hear spirits, raise and reanimate the dead, prolong life and heal.'

'I haven't shown any signs of any of those things. Then again I didn't show signs of having any power until a couple of days ago and even then it was only when you showed me how.'

'You did when you were little, that's why we moved away from here. Just because you haven't shown any signs of it yet doesn't mean anything. You haven't had your ceremony, both your power and your memories are still bound. I don't think you realise how powerful you're going to be.' Mum said with a worried look on her face.

'It'll be fine. You worry too much.' I said.

'Only because I know you. You run head first into danger, you're every Mother's worst nightmare.'

'Ha thanks Mum. I have realised that I've lead a sheltered life, everything here is new and interesting. I'm sure things will settle down soon.'

'I hope so,' she responded. 'So what about you and Adam? You seem to be getting along.' she asked.

'What is this? You are the second person to say that to me today. Me and Adam are just friends.'

'Leona and I have always had this fantasy when you were little that you and Adam would grow up and get married. I was just wondering if that was coming true.'

'Keep dreaming Mum.' I said.

'Mm-hmm.' Was all she said in response.

CHAPTER 11

I t was time. My ceremony was about to start. I was dressed in a knee length silver dress that Fiona helped me pick out with my gorgeous new robe on top. She had also came by and helped with my hair and makeup. I had two little plaits tied together at the back of my head and the rest of my long blonde hair was down and wavy.

There were so many people here, half of them I didn't know, I spotted Adam and Lucas in the crowd, Adam winked at me. Everyone was situated within the stone circle talking in whispers, the sconces burning on the stones shedding an eerie light about the clearing. I was shaking like a leaf. I walked carrying my bowls with my offerings, unsteadily into the middle of the stone circle and knelt on the cushion provided under the Blackthorn tree in front of High Priest David. As I knelt the whispering came to a halt. I set the bowls down and looked up at David expectantly.

'Druid brothers and sisters, I welcome you all here today to share in Ashton's new beginning, as a fully fledged Druid. Many years have passed since we have seen Ashton, but we welcome her home with open arms as a member of our Grove. Ashton, I want you to repeat after me.' I nodded.

I call upon our ancestors on the twilight eve of my twenty fifth year
Please accept my humble offerings of thanks for the legacy

of power that you have passed down to me throughout the
generations and the power you lend me in the face of our foes.
I accept my sacred duty, to protect my fellow
Druids and our lands from harm.
I will be one with nature, through Earth, Water,
Fire and Air I shall honour and serve you.
So mote it be.

I repeated after David, the air felt charged, I felt like our ancestors were here with us, giving me their blessing, it was a much more emotional experience than what I expected. When I finished speaking, the rest of the gathered crowd chanted, 'So mote it be.' over and over again. The charge in the air seemed to become an unbearable weight pressing down on me until suddenly, it was like the dam had broke, the earth shook, it started to rain, the flames of the sconces soared higher than the blackthorn tree and a mini tornado seemed to appear from thin air right in front of me, and then I heard a voice, 'Of course they left us out, bloody conceited Druids.' I looked around to try and find where the voice was coming from but the wind whipped my hair about my face, and then I heard the faint echo of far away voices say 'So mote it be.' as I was struck by an invisible force right in my centre where my magic stems from, knocking the wind right out of me and then just like that, it all stopped, the tornado disappeared, the rain stopped, the fire went out and the earth stilled. I looked around me expectantly, wondering where the voice that had seemed to be right next to me had came from. But there was no one there other than David.

Immediately everyone started chattering again only more loudly this time than before. 'Well that was a first,' David mumbled. Then louder he shouted over the din to be heard, 'Well done Ashton, you done beautifully, that was certainly the most eventful ceremony I have ever attended. Let me help you up.'

He helped me to my feet. I was grateful for the robe that had kept me mostly dry. Everyone got in a line, apparently to shake my hand, to hug me, welcome me or give me some other words of wisdom, I was mortified. Funny how no one told me about this part I thought. When Adam got to me, he said 'Holy shit Ashton, I thought you were going to blow us all up, that was epic.' I laughed at Adam's complete inappropriateness to the situation. When the line moved along to Fiona, she gave me a hug. 'Welcome Ashton, I'm so glad you're here.' My mum and my Granny both gave me a hug and told me they were proud of me.

Lucas was at the very end of the line, as he reached me, he bent to give me a kiss on the cheek and wrapped one of his hands around my wrist, reminding me of last night, as his lips touched my cheek I got that electric shock sensation again, it was so abrupt that it momentarily made me light headed. 'Well done, you were amazing.' He whispered into my ear. I was so dumbstruck I didn't manage to utter a word before he set off after everyone else to the barn that my Granny had decorated specially for my after ceremony party.

David walked beside me to the barn. 'You are officially one of us Ashton, I'm so glad to have you here, I know it's made your Grandmother very happy.'

'Thanks, I'm happy to be here too.'

When I went into the barn I couldn't get over how good it looked, it definitely didn't look like a barn inside. There were lots of fairy lights hung everywhere, there were tables laid with table cloths and lots of party food and even better lots of alcohol. I left David's side and went straight over to get myself a glass of prosecco. There I was set upon by my cousins, Jacob, Anna and Caitlyn. 'You look amazing Ashton, its so good to see you.' Caitlyn said.

'Thank you, and thanks for coming for my ceremony Caitlyn. I'm sure it was a long drive from Kerry.'

'Six hours with all the stopping and starting, snack breaks, toilet breaks, you know how it goes. I wouldn't have missed it though. Ian is at home with the boys. I'm just glad to get some peace, this is like a holiday for me.' I laughed. Caitlyn was married to a Druid from County Kerry and had 2 boys under the age of 5.

'Caitlyn, stop hogging Ashton,' Anna said. 'That was really something with your ceremony. I've never seen anything like it.'

'I wouldn't know, that was my first ceremony, so I wasn't really sure what to expect.' I replied.

'Well for future reference, not that.' she laughed. Anna lived not far from Bushmills in Coleraine, she was about to finish her final year of uni studying a degree in biology. She was younger than the rest of the cousins at 21 so she hadn't had her own ceremony yet. Caitlyn and Anna were Aunt Emma and Uncle Mark's daughters.

Jacob came and gave me a tight hug, 'Hey cus, good to see you.' Jacob was Uncle Malcolm and Aunt Patricia's son. Aunt Patricia wasn't a Druid, so she gave these types of things a wide berth.

We all caught up talking and laughing. It was great to see all of my cousins, although we didn't see a lot of eachother growing up they were always kind to me and seemed happy to see me. Fiona, Adam and Lucas joined us. Fiona and Jacob seemed to be getting along very well. When I seen my Mum giving me the eyes, I thought I better mingle, after all, everyone was here for me.

I talked to Diane and Richard Clarke who live just a few houses down from us and their grownup kids, Jamie and Alexis. Then to Darryl and Courtney Johnston who also lived nearby and Elaine and Martin Young, who were good friend's of Grannys. Everyone was lovely but I was starting to get a bit of a headache. As the night wore on, it got harder and harder to ignore, so I switched from Prosecco to water.

'Ashton, are you alright? You look awful pale.' it was Granny, she was passing me to go talk to the Youngs, but paused when she seen me.

'I'm ok, I've just got the worst headache.' I said touching my forehead, which felt hot and I was grateful for the coolness of my hand.

'I think maybe you should go to bed, between your ceremony and the unbinding, I should have guessed that you would feel a little under the weather.'

'But what about the guests, would that not be a bit rude?' I asked.

'It's ok, don't you worry about it, it's getting late anyway. Just come inside with me first and I'll get you something for that headache.' she lead me into the house leaving no room for argument.

I thought she would give me 2 paracetamol, but instead, she boiled the kettle and got out an old fashioned mortal and pestle and started crushing up some herbs from little jars and when the kettle was ready she poured the boiled water in and mixed it all up, then poured it in a cup for me. 'Drink it.' she ordered handing me the cup. I blew on the steaming mixture afraid of burning myself, but more afraid of disobeying Granny, so I took a sip, it was warm but it had a pleasant taste, like mint and ginger. I drank it slowly allowing it to cool down slightly. When I have finished, my headache had eased a little but I still felt hot and beyond tired.

'I think I'm going to go up to bed Granny, thanks for the - tea?' I said questioningly.

'You go on ahead dear. I'll let everyone know where you've got to.'

I went upstairs to bed, I took my shoes off and my robe, but that was all I could manage. I was shivering so I got into bed in my dress as quickly as I could and pulled my quilt right up to under my chin and closed my eyes. My head pounded, I thought I would never get to sleep but before I knew it I was dreaming.

I dreamt that I was a little girl playing in the fields out the back of the house with Adam, he was adorable as a kid, with his dark floppy hair curling around his face and forehead, piercing green eyes and long eyelashes. I was holding a kite and running with it, he was running along side me trying to jump and catch the kite. I toppled over from running and paying more attention to the kite than where my feet were going, I began to cry, but Adam was there, holding out his chubby little hand to help me up, whilst telling me that it was ok, and asking where was hurt because he would kiss it better.

The dream changed, I was in my Granny's kitchen sobbing over a napkin with a little mouse on it, that lay unmoving, the mouse twitched, but I couldn't see because I was crying so hard, Adam was telling me to stop crying because the mouse was ok, I looked up as the mouse rolled onto its front and stared in amazement as it got up and ran along the table.

The dream changed again and Granny and I where in the field out back, she clicked her fingers and a flame shot out of her thumb like I had seen her do before and then she blew it out, only this time, I copied her, it took me a few goes to click my fingers and a flame shot out of my thumb too and I blew it out and squealed with delight. Granny gave me a hug and spun me around, 'Well done, you are remarkable little one.'

I looked up and then I was in my bedroom, only it was different. It was still decorated in blues with soft greys in place of silvers and there was toy box with my name carved into it and my bed was smaller, maybe it just seemed like that because it was filled with teddy bears, Uncle Malcolm was there too, he was reading me a story from a book, the cover read 'The Guardians of the Enchanted Grove'.

The scene before me flickered over and over again, me and Adam playing together, me sticking a pencil in Adam's ear and him crying and me comforting him whilst crying too, hugging my Mum outside my nursery school and crying because I didn't want to leave her, Mum bathing me whilst I used my water magic to splash her, playing with my cousins in the fields, picking strawberrys with my cousin Jacob and eating them all, Jacob pulling my hair because I ate the last one, me crying because Jacob pulled my hair, Jacob crying because I used my air magic to slap his cheek, me talking to Great Great Granny Sadie and her telling me to tell Granny Thelma that she puts too many onions in her stew, Mum crying because we had to leave, on and on and on it went, a never ending stream of dreams, until I woke up.

When I woke up, I felt something cold and damp on my forehead. I opened my eyes and as they adjusted to the light they met Adams green eyes staring back at me with the strangest look on his face, it was strange because it was a serious look, concern, something I'd never seen from Adam before. 'Hey, you're ok now,' Adam said softly, 'you're ok.' I then realised he was holding a cloth to my forehead.

I pushed up on my elbows and straightened up in bed, he was still holding onto the cloth. 'What's wrong?' I asked.

'Ashton, you've been delirious for the past 12 hours, you've had a really high fever and were shouting out in your sleep, everyone's been really worried. Your Mum has only just left a couple of hours ago, at my insistence that she get some rest.' I took in Adam's dishevelled appearance.

'It's ok, I feel alright.' I said as much for my benefit as for his, 'I was having so many weird dreams. It must have been the fever.'

'Your Granny thinks that your memories flooding back plus the unbinding of your powers due to the ceremony may have caused this. Here she gave me this and told me to get you to drink it when you woke up.' He lifted a mug and held it to my lips, the liquid inside smelt fowl and tasted even worse. I coughed a gulp down, 'Jesus, is she trying to kill me?'

He laughed, 'I'm not sure what was in that but it did smell gross. She said it would make you feel better though.' He held it up for me to take another drink, I held my nose first and then gulped the rest down as quickly as I could so I wouldn't have to taste it. He moved the cup away and brushed my hair back from my face, I looked at him, suddenly very aware of how close he was. 'I'm glad you're ok.' he said, 'Oh and by the way, happy birthday.'

'No way, I can't believe I forgot it was my birthday!' I exclaimed.

'I got you a present.'

'Really? You didn't have to do that, but since you already went to the trouble, I accept.' I said.

He laughed, 'Hang on a minute and I'll go get it, and also let everyone know you're ok.' he said getting up to leave.

'Thanks for staying with me Adam.'

'It's ok, I didn't have anything better to do.' he joked.

CHAPTER 12

The next thing I knew I was surrounded by Mum, Granny, Aunt Emma, Uncle Mark, Uncle Malcolm, Jacob, Caitlyn, Anna, Leona and Adam. They all had birthday presents for me too. It was like a party in my bedroom.

'How are you? Are you feeling better sweetheart?' Mum asked. 'Adam insisted I go to sleep for a while, I only left because he agreed to wake me the moment you were awake. As soon as we realised you were sick, he refused to leave your side the whole night. I'm sure he's exhausted.'

'I'm ok, thanks. That gross stuff I had to drink has definitely helped clear my head a bit. I still feel a little shivery. How did you know I was sick?' I asked.

'Granny told me you had went to bed because you weren't feeling great so I came to check on you and you were talking and mumbling in your sleep, and you had kicked your covers off and were running a fever.' She lifted my tangled mass of hair and dropped it again, and it suddenly dawned on me what I must look like lying here, I quickly flatten my hair down with my hands. I could see Adam looking whilst laughing behind his hand that was covering his mouth. He removed his hand and said 'Your hair is lovely Ashton.' I threw my pillow at him.

'Thank you all so much for coming to check on me and bring

me birthday presents but I really am ok. Would you mind if I got a quick shower and then I'll come downstairs and open my presents?'

Everyone filed out. Adam and my Mum stayed behind, 'Are you sure you're ok? Adam asked.

'Yes I'm fine Adam, I'll be down soon.'

'Ok, if you're sure.' he replied.

'I'm sure, thanks Adam.'

When he left my Mum turned to look at me eyes wide, 'What's not to love?'

'Muuumm' I groaned.

She laughed,'Ok ok. Now are you really ok?'

'I think so, I still feel a little feverish and weak, but not bad enough to waste the rest of my birthday laying in bed.' I grinned.

'Ok, lets see you get up then. I sat completely upright in bed and turned to let my legs dangle over the edge of the bed. I felt a little light headed but I wasn't going to admit that to my Mum. 'I had loads of dreams last night, but I realised it was my memories coming back. It must have been really hard for you leaving here and your whole family and you did all of that just to keep me safe.'

My Mum looked at me softly, 'Of course I did sweetheart.'

'Thank you.' I said.

'Come on stop stalling, I thought you were going to get ready, lets see you stand up.' she said changing the subject.

I got up and although I was a little unsteady on my feet, on the whole I actually felt better than expected, and my headache was gone so that was a bonus. Once my Mum was happy that I was ok she left and went downstairs to allow me to get a shower.

I felt much better after showering. I went downstairs and everyone was in the sitting room, David had obviously arrived whilst I was getting ready and Mia was with him too. I guess Mum was right about David never being too far from Granny.

'Oh good you fixed your hair.' Adam said as I walked into the room. I looked around for something to throw at him, but finding nothing that wasn't breakable I just laughed instead.

Everyone gave me presents, it was so nice to have my whole family around me, especially on my birthday instead of just me and Mum. It was one of the nicest birthdays I've had.

When I thought I'd opened all of my presents Adam came and handed me a long slim blue suede box, 'Here, this is for you.' It looked like there might be jewellery or something inside and I could feel my face getting red just at the thought of opening it in front of everyone.

'Thanks Adam.' I smiled at him, wishing I could open it later. I went to set it on the coffee table beside me, but Adam wasn't having any of it, 'Aren't you going to open it?'

'Er, yeah sure.' I said not wanting to offend him.

I slowly opened the box, not knowing what to expect. I should have known better than to think it was jewellery. Inside was a really, really sharp pencil. As I looked at it, I looked up at Adam and we both burst out laughing. We were getting some confused looks, so I held the pencil up so everyone could see and we all cracked up laughing. It was even funnier now that I had that memory back. Adam left out the part of the story where he tried to stick the pencil up my nose first so I grabbed it off him and shoved it in his ear.

After a while I went and sat next to Mia who had been awfully quiet. 'Hi, how are you doing?' I asked.

She rolled her eyes, 'I'm fine.'

'Sick of everyone asking you that?' I asked.

'Pretty much.' she smiled wryly.

'Well how about I help you come up with a plan to get Sophia back rather than sympathising with you.' I said.

Mia looked back at me in shock. 'Are you serious? Why would you want to help get Sophia back after what she done to you?'

'Because I think by now she probably realises she has made a huge mistake, and I hate to think of what the necromancers will do her. I don't think she deserves to be left to her fate with them because of one mistake.'

'You're a better person than I am. She's my sister and even I go back and forth on the idea of helping her. But I also don't know how to help her, what can we do?'

'My Mum said that it's your Granda David's decision as the High Priest of our Grove. I think we should try and gather support amongst her friends and go to him and ask for permission and help with a rescue mission of sorts.'

'That could work, though that's based on getting support from other Druid's, which will prove more difficult. My Mum has disowned her, she is so angry with her and ashamed of what she has done, I don't think she will agree to help.' Mia replied hopelessly.

'Why don't you let me deal with your Mum? Sometimes it's better coming from someone who isn't so close to the situation.' I said.

'I still can't believe you would really do this for my sister.'

'I just hope she's ok and they haven't decided already that she's no longer useful to them. Give me your phone number and we can meet tomorrow and try and find some friends who are willing to support Sophia.'

'Thank you, Ashton.' Mia said then I handed her my phone to put in her number.

After that we got a chinese takeaway for dinner. I felt so much better, even if I ate way too much, I was actually glad Adam kept stealing food from my plate as it stopped me from eating it all. When we were done, Adam asked me did I want to go for a walk to work some of the food off. We went out through the back of the house, past the clearing and down the lane that was between the fields. It was still light out at this time of year.

The lane was slightly overgrown with weeds and wild flowers and seemed to go on for miles. Beyond the fields was a forest, the further we walked the more overgrown it became.

'How are you feeling now?' Adam asked as we walked.

'I actually feel pretty good.' I said surprising myself.

'Good enough to practice some magic?' he asked with a sideways grin at me.

'What do you have in mind?' I asked.

'I'll show you.' he said marching on ahead of me. The lane eventually forked and we took the path to the left into another huge clearing which held the Castle. There were two large stone statues depicting a cloaked man and women, that I presumed were druids. It was in much better condition than the ruins in Dunluce, although it wasn't even close to Dunluce castle in size. At least it had a roof though and was modern enough to have windows. It looked kind of like an old church, with stained glass windows and a steeple. Ivy had grown up the walls, some of the windows were broken where it had grown through. It was pretty awesome.

Adam stopped in the middle of the clearing and turned back to see if I was still following, I was too busy looking around me in awe. 'Hey, you coming?' he said.

'Yes, this is just so cool. I only remember coming here once before when I was little.'

'I always loved it here too. Come on he said, he walked me around to the back of the steeple to where there was a door, then he turned the handle and opened it. Inside there was another door, leading into the castle and then a steep spiral stone staircase. He started to climb up, but I stopped him. 'Wait, where are you going?' I asked.

'Come on, you'll see.'

Reluctantly I followed him, up and up we went, until I was breathless and sweating and my thigh muscles burned. When we reached the top there was a belfry, it seemed strange that this would be up here. The bell took up the whole middle section of the floor and there was only a small amount of space around the perimeter in which we could walk. The outer walls reached just below my shoulders. There was a little ledge slightly lower down that I stood on to look further over the edge. In one corner was a ladder that lead to a loft. 'Hey, up here.' Adam said climbing the old wooden ladder. I followed behind him. The space wasn't very big, but there was enough room for us both to stand upright. There was a large window in one side that opened outwards onto a stone ledge that went all the way around the steeple.

'What are we doing up here?' I asked, a bit miffed of how he was going to show me how to use my magic up here.

'Watch and see.' was all he said as he stood on up on the ledge surrounding us and jumped, I screamed, 'Adam!' my heart was in my throat as I ran to the ledge and looked down and there was Adam, laughing and floating with his hands behind his head.. 'What the fuck Adam? I thought you'd just jumped to your death. How are you doing that?' I ranted at him.

He laughed again, 'I'm using my air magic. I thought you might like to try it.'

'Are you actually crazy? I'm not jumping off a fucking building the first time I use my air magic. I think we need to start smaller.'

'Oh come on, I won't let you fall, don't you trust me?'

'You're away in the head if you think I'm going to jump off this roof. Now come back in, you're making me nervous.'

He cackled with laughter, 'Aww it's nice to know you care so much.' he said as he suddenly dropped lower, I leant over the edge with my arm outstretched to him.

'Adam, this isn't even funny, I'm going to leave right now if you don't come back in.'

He slowly floated back up towards me and over the ledge and when he was in position he straightened his legs and dropped lightly to the ground.

'Let me show you, close your eyes.' he said.

I glared at him and he just smiled serenely back at me, then I reluctantly closed my eyes. 'Feel for your magic but don't pull on it yet. Once you've found it, try and pull on the individual strands to find the one you want to use. Each different strand of magic should have a different sensation, so you can tell them apart. At first you will need to concentrate to tell which one is which, but with a bit of practice it will just come naturally to you.'

I took a deep breath and felt low down near my belly button for my magic, I tried not to pull on it, but the ground started to shake. Adam chuckled, 'Easy there, you're just trying to find it. What you just pulled on was your earth magic, so try and pull on another strand, hold your hand out palm up as you do it.'

I tried again, this time immediately finding the strand of my earth magic which in my imagination was green, and pushed it to the side, then pulled on the next strand which was blue, little beads of water came out from the cracks in the stone on the ground and formed a pool of water in my hand. Then I pushed the strand away again and pulled on the red one, a flame shot up from my hand this time, I opened my eyes in surprise. This was so easy compared to the other times I'd called on my magic. I pushed the red strand away and finally I pulled on the white strand and a mini tornado formed in the palm of my hand. Then I let it go an just as quickly as it had started it all stopped.

I let out a breath I didn't realise I was holding. 'That was so cool.'

'I knew you'd pick it up quickly.' he smiled. 'Now that you've found your air magic, I want you to try again, only this time I want you to imagine you're pushing the air to the ground beneath your feet.'

I done as he said, I closed my eyes and found my magic and pulled on the white strand this time pushing it down my legs, to my feet, then my toes and then beyond to the ground, I felt a small gust of wind from beneath me and I gasped as my feet lifted off the ground, I nearly let go of the white air magic in my shock, I wobbled a little and then straightened up again, I opened my eyes and looked down and I was floating a few inches off the ground. 'Holy shit, I did it.' As I said it I lost my concentration and wobbled again, as Adam caught my arm and held on until I straightened up.

'Not bad, now for the real test. Push the air up through your feet to gain more height, then try and hold it. See if you can get your feet higher than the ledge.'

I took a deep breath and done as he said, I was a little wobbly at first but once I figured out where to position the air to keep my balance I was much more steady.

'Ok now try and push yourself forwards towards me.' he said taking a couple of steps back.

I tried to push the air up through the back of my feet to push myself forwards, but instead I pushed myself up into the air then quickly fell forward on top of Adam knocking him off his feet onto his back, all the while I was shrieking. We hit the ground together with a thud. I pushed up on my hands and my hair fell into his face, I pulled it back out of the way over my shoulder and our eyes met and we both burst out laughing. 'Well that was a great success.' I said trying to back back up on my feet.

'You need to push forward whilst holding yourself upright, so you want the air underneath your feet steady, and the air behind you to push you forward. Try again, you can do it.' he said whilst getting to his feet and brushing himself off.

I took a few steps back from him and tried again, I pulled on the white strand of my magic and pushed it down through my feet until I lifted smoothly off the ground, once I felt completely balanced, I pulled the air behind me and used it to push myself forward, and then gently eased off just before I reached Adam. I smiled, delighted with myself, then pulled the air back around to the front of me and used it to push myself backwards, then to a stop again. I was grinning now.

'You're such a show off.' Adam said smirking. 'Are you brave enough to step off the ledge now?'

I nodded then I pushed myself up until I was level with the ledge and stood on it, I took a deep breath and then began to think about what I was about to do, if I fell from here there would be no coming back from it. I went to take a step then hesitated and wobbled, Adam grabbed me around the waist and steadied me. He climbed up onto the ledge beside me and took me by the hand, 'It's ok, we can do it together, I won't let you fall.' He

looked at me and I nodded at him and we stepped off together, I
didn't even need to think about it, it just came naturally, mostly
because it would be stupid to die when I knew how to float. The
air pushed up beneath my feet, strong and steady. I was still
holding on to Adam's hand as he turned towards me. 'Lets move
further away from the ledge. Just how I showed you.' We pushed
forward together, it felt a bit like flying upright, our hands joined
together were like a wing. I held my other arm out to the side,
just to balance myself. My hair blew around me, the air felt cool
against my skin. It was the most amazing sensation.

'This is so cool.' I said over the noise of the wind.

Adam looked down, 'Are you ready to go down?'

I looked at him panicked.

'It's ok, all you need to do is hold on to me, let go of your air magic
and pull on it again when we're about 20 feet from the ground,
then gently release it to lower yourself to your feet. I won't let
anything happen to you. Ok?'

'Ok.' I said more confidently than I felt. Internally I was freaking
out.
'Ok, you ready?' I gulped and nodded.

'Release your magic now.' and I did release it. I felt weightless but
I was falling.

I couldn't help but look down, I started to panic but then Adam
squeezed my hand. I could hear the wind whip past my ears.
Adam shouted "Pull on your magic'. I did, as he said, I wrapped
my magic around myself like a cushion. I felt like I was floating
again. When I looked down this time I was about 10ft from
the ground, I slowly and steadily released the air from beneath
me and lowered myself to the ground. When I was just above
the ground I straightened my legs out underneath me to allow
myself to stand, as I did though I lost concentration and let go

completely, landing on my feet with a thud and immediately falling forward onto my knees and letting go of Adam's hand. But my knees never touched the ground. It was like I'd landed on a cushion - Adam.

'Another graceful landing.' Adam laughed.

'Thanks. That was amazing. I can't believe I just did that.' I said looking up at how far we had dropped from the top of the steeple.

'You did great. I knew you could do it. It comes so naturally to you. I didn't learn to do that until I was 18 and I'd been using my magic since I was a little kid.' Adam said in awe.

'Are you kidding me?' I said shoving him, 'What if I fell to my death?' I fumed standing up as he held out his hand to help me, I took it reluctantly.

'I wouldn't have let anything happen to you, I knew you were safe or I wouldn't have tried.' he said seriously. Somehow we were now face to face and my hand was still in his and he was looking at me expectantly.

I broke the silence, 'Well I will forgive you this time, since I lived.' He still didn't speak, I was sure he was going to kiss me and I couldn't decide if I wanted him to or not.

'Hey there you are.' A voice broke me out of the trance I was in and I took a step back from Adam and turned around to see Fiona waving at us and Lucas walking alongside her looking angry.

'Hey, what are you guys doing here?' I said, feeling guilty like I'd done something wrong.

'We came to wish you a happy birthday.' Fiona replied, 'Oh and to bring you a present, though it's back at the house.'

'Thank you, you didn't need to do that.' I said.

'It's not every day you turn 25, that's a big deal for Druids. Anyway what are you's doing here?'

'We just came for a walk after dinner and Adam was showing me how to use my air magic. It was awesome. We just half floated, half fell from the top of the steeple.'

'Are you crazy? What if something had happened to you?' Lucas said looking furious now.

'Hi to you too Lucas.' was all I said in response.

'Oh give over Lucas, would you.' Fiona said. He just scowled even more in response. 'That sounds really cool, I always wished I had air magic so I could fly.' she replied to me. 'Go on then, show us.' I looked up at Lucas but he said nothing. Then I said to Adam 'You coming?'

We walked to the back of the steeple then through the door again. 'Is Lucas always like that?' I asked.

Adam seemed thoughtful for a second, then said 'No not usually, you seem to bring it out in him. It's obvious that he likes you.'

'You told me that already, so did Fiona.' I replied.

'Is the feeling mutual?' he asked cautiously.

'I don't know why everyone keeps saying he likes me.' I said avoiding the question.

'Oh come on Ashton, it's plain for everyone to see. You didn't answer my question.' he said sounding annoyed.

'I don't really know him all that well, he can nice but he can also be really intense, like just now. I'm not really sure what to make of him to be honest.' I talked as we continued up the steep winding steps of the steeple, with Adam walking behind me. I couldn't tell Adam that I also wasn't sure if I could trust him, because he was the only other person who knew about the book and it was stolen. Suddenly Adam grabbed my arm and stopped me walking any further. 'What are you doing?' I asked.

He turned me to face him, I was almost the same height as him, standing on the step above him. He was so close I could feel his breath on my cheek. He sucked in a breath and then exhaled, 'I just it want to be clear, in case you're totally oblivious, that I like you. I don't expect anything from you, I get that everything has changed for you very quickly, so I won't rush you, but I just want you to consider me. Will you think about it?' he looked me right in the eyes and I nodded totally taken aback and lost for words.

He smiled, 'Relax, we're good. Let's get a move on, they'll be wondering what's taking us so long.'

I exhaled and we made the rest of the journey up the steep steps in silence, while I reeled in shock at Adam's revelation that he likes me. I had loved Adam since I was little but we had spent so much time apart, I had to get to know him again. Obviously he was gorgeous, and funny, we always had a good time, but he also had a more serious side, he had shown me that in the way he had looked after me and worrried about me. There was so much happening at once, I'm glad he wasn't rushing me, because I wasn't sure I was ready to think about this at the moment.

We reached the top and climbed up the ladder and onto the ledge. I waved down at Fiona and Lucas. Fiona cupped her hands together and yelled 'Don't die on us.'

I laughed 'Thanks for the vote of confidence.' I muttered.

'You ready?' Adam asked holding out his hand for me to hold.

I smiled and took his hand. 'Lets do it.'

We stepped off the ledge together pushing the air under us to hold us steady, then pushed forward clear of the ledge. He turned to me and nodded. We both released our air magic, using just enough to control our fall. We dropped fast, the wind blowing my hair in my face, I could hear Fiona whooping and cheering somewhere beneath me, I kept my grip on Adam's hand afraid to let go, he shouted above the wind, 'Now Ashton.' I pushed the air up beneath me like a cushion again and gently eased off until I was nearly at the ground then set my feet down, thankfully perfecting the landing this time and saving myself the embarassment of falling in front of Lucas and Fiona.

'That was amazing.' Fiona said.

'It was pretty cool.' Lucas said smiling at me now. Jeez make up your mind.

'Are you ready to go back now?' Fiona asked, 'I'm excited for you to open your present.'

I laughed, 'Sure lets go. So what is it?' I asked.

'You'll just have to be patient.'

When we got back to the house we went into the kitchen and Fiona pulled me by the hand into the games room. There were two wrapped presents and a box sitting on the pool table waiting for me. 'Open them, open them, open them.' She was practically bouncing.

I laughed, 'Ok give me a chance.' I said walking to the pool table. Adam raised his eyebrow at me, Lucas smiled. I ripped the blue and silver wrapping paper in a frenzy like a kid, and inside was a gorgeous blue halter neck dress that flowed out from just below the bust and had silver sequins attached to the skirt. 'I love it, thank you Fiona.'

'Yay, I knew you'd love it, now open the other one.' I don't know who was more excited, Fiona or me.

I ripped open the other present and inside was a pair of silver strappy sandals with bigger heels than I had ever worn. They perfectly complimented the dress. 'These are gorgeous, though I'm not sure I'll be able to walk in them.'

'They are supposed to go with the dress. Go put them on, I'm going to get ready too.' Fiona said.

'Erm ready for what?' I asked.

Lucas started laughing, 'In her excitement my sister forgot to tell you, we have planned a night out for you.'

Adam laughed now too. 'I hope I'm invited.'

'Of course mate.' Lucas said.

'So is anyone going to tell me where we're going?'

'Halo in Ballycastle.' Fiona said expectantly, like it should mean something to me.

'Am I supposed to know where that is? I'm not from around here, remember?'

'Sorry I forgot, it's a nightclub, sometimes they have live bands or dj's or cocktail nights, but tonight they're having an Old Skool UV Party.'

'Sounds good, what time are we going?' I asked.

'Is an hour enough time for you to get ready?' Fiona replied.

'Sure.'

Chapter 13

Just over an hour and a half and a few proseccos later, we were ready and getting into a taxi to Halo. I was excited about this impromptu night out. Then I had a thought. 'Hey did anyone ask Mia if she wanted to come?'

'I didn't even think to ask her, I guess I didn't think she would be feeling up to it after everything that's happened.' Fiona said.

'I suppose so. I wanted to talk to you guys about something. I have arranged to meet up with Mia tomorrow to try and gather support among the other Druids to attempt a rescue mission for Sophia.' I said whispering the last part about Druids so the taxi driver didn't hear me over the radio. Though he didn't seem to be paying attention anyway.

'You what now?' It was Adam that spoke. 'You better be fucking joking Ashton. That bitch tried to have you captured.'

'Look, I get where you're coming from but she made a mistake. Does she deserve to live with the consequences of that for the rest of her life, however long that might be. Who knows what the necromancers might do to her. I'm guessing that by now, shes already regretting her decision.'

'You are just the cutest,' Fiona said, I guessed she was already a bit tipsy.

'I agree with Ashton.' Lucas said. 'Whilst I'm angry about what she done, I think she was probably mislead by the necromancers. I think she deserves another chance, providing she is sorry for what she's done.'

'The necromancers could have done anything to you Ashton, they could of murdered you, she knew that and she didn't care. She just wanted you out of the way and now you want to help her? I think you're mad.'

'Well, I still want to try. If anyone wants to help they can, if you don't then I won't force you, but I'm doing what feels right to me.'

'I'll think about it.' Adam said.

'I'll help.' Lucas and Fiona said at once.

'You're doing that creepy twin thing again.' I laughed. 'Lets forget about it for tonight anyway, I just want to enjoy tonight.'

'Agreed.' Adam said. 'We're almost there anyway.' he pointed up ahead.

We pulled up outside Halo. The building was painted a pale blue on the outside, so there was no missing it. We paid the taxi driver and got out. My new shoes were way more comfortable than expected. They were a good choice. They matched perfectly with my blue dress, which came to just above my knee. I felt taller than I usually did which was always a bonus. Even still I was a little wobbly on my feet, still adjusting to the extra height. Lucas put his hand on my arm to steady me as I walked along the pavement into the nightclub. Inside the ceiling was covered in dangling disco balls and uv lights, it was packed, people were dancing, their white teeth glowing under the UV light, people had glow sticks and were waving them around and other people who were wearing all white, were lit up like a glo fish. It looked awesome. Lucas pushed his way ahead towards the bar, Fiona grabbed me by the wrist and trailed me along behind her to the bar whilst Adam pushed his way through beside us. Lucas bought us all a drink. We found a table and a couple of bar stools off to the side of the dance floor. It was so loud, we couldn't hear eachother speak so there was nothing left to do but dance.

Fiona, Adam and I hit the dance floor. It took me a minute to realise Lucas hadn't came with us. I looked back to see Lucas standing at our table watching us. He smiled. I left Fiona and Adam to go and talk to him. 'What's wrong, have you got 2 left feet?' I teased.

'I don't know, I just don't really dance. You go ahead, I'm happy to watch you all and look after our drinks.'

'That's no fun.' I said. I lifted my prosecco and downed it in one. 'There's no need to stay here if there are no drinks to watch, drink up.' I watched as he lifted his beer and downed it,then set the empty bottle down. He smiled at me then I took him by the hand and turned pulling him along with me, I half expected him to resist, but he came willingly.

When we reached Fiona and Adam, Adam was looking slightly annoyed, remembering our earlier conversation I could guess why, but I wasn't going to let Lucas stand alone whilst we all enjoyed ourselves. Fiona shouted something in my ear that I couldn't hear then smiled and started waving her arms around above her head and dancing to the music and Adam joined in. I looked at Lucas who was looking back at me, he stuck out like a sore thumb he was so big and bulky and he was standing there in his plain black t-shirt and jeans looking broody on the dance floor while everyone was dancing and jumping all around him. I grabbed his hands and got that now familiar zing of an electric shock that I always seemed to get when we touched, he looked at me in surprise, but I moved his hands with mine and starting dancing and jumping around like everyone else, he soon joined in and was laughing, seeing Adam's glare I let go of one of Lucas's hands and took one of Adam's, he smiled at me and took Fiona's hand with his spare hand. Soon we were all dancing in our own little circle having the best time. I couldn't help but notice both Adam and Lucas glancing at me every time I looked up. After the end of another song, we went to get more drinks, Adam got them this time and Fiona and I went to the ladies.

'Looks like you have a decision to make Ashton.'she said going to check her makeup in the mirror.
'What do you mean?' I asked confused.
'Well it's clear both Adam and my brother like you. I'm just a third wheel or fourth wheel should I say in this whole scenario.' she laughed.

I groaned, 'Please don't say that. I've no idea if your brother likes me or not, but Adam has already made it clear how he feels and I don't want to upset anyone, I just want to enjoy the night and not think about it or feel pressured. I really don't know either of them very well anyway.'

'What do you mean Adam made it clear how he feels?' Fiona asked shocked and clearly desperate to know everything.

'He told me earlier tonight that he likes me but he won't rush me.'

'Oh my ggggooooddd. Isn't he the sweetest?' she all but swooned.

I laughed, 'Yeah I guess it is kind of nice and I'm also grateful for the breathing space, but I also sort of wish I didn't know, because even if he isn't rushing me, I can't help but feel pressured. Especially because everyone keeps telling me Lucas likes me too.' I don't know where all that came from.

'Oh Ashton, I'm sorry. I was just getting carried away. I'm definitely drunk. Lets just go and have a good time.'

'Ok, I just need to use the bathroom first.' I grumbled.

The boys were waiting with drinks when we got back. 'Thanks,' I raised my glass of prosecco

and nodded at Adam and downed it in one again, determined
  that no one was going to spike my drink
and it was my birthday so I could do what I wanted. Adam raised
  his eyebrows at me and downed his
beer as well and Fiona and Lucas followed suit.

'Oh, I have an idea, lets get some shots.' Fiona said excitedly and
  clapped her hands.

'Is that a good idea?' Lucas asked, always the sensible one.

'Absolutely, come on.' I grinned and grabbed Fiona by the wrist
  and pulled her to the bar with me and left the boys to it.

'So what will we get?' I asked Fiona when we were at the bar,
  waiting to be served.

'I like sambuca, but it doesn't like me. What do you like? Jager-
  bombs, Tequilla, Cola cubes? Absinthe? ' she asked.

'I think like is a strong word to use, but I've never had a Jager-
  bomb before.'

'No way, ok you definitely have to have a Jager-bomb then. I'll get
  them, put your purse away.' she said waving my hand away.

'It's ok I'll get them, thank you for bringing me here tonight it's
  been fun.' I said.

She gave me a one armed hug 'I'm just glad you're here, and it's
your birthday so I'm buying and before you try to argue, don't. I
want to be able to say I bought you your first Jager-bomb.'

I laughed, 'Can't argue with that.'

She bought 4 Jager Bombs and the bar man gave us a tray to

carry them back to our table on. A Jager-bomb was half a glass of red bull with a shot of jagermeister dropped inside. When we got to the table Adam cheered, lifted his glass and downed it in one. Lucas shook his head, but he wasn't going to be outdone, so he lifted his glass and done the same. Fiona and I clinked glasses and drank ours at the same time, the shot glass inside the taller glass hit off my teeth. My chest burned and I made a face and coughed and Adam and Lucas laughed. 'So what did you think?' Fiona asked.

'It was ok as shots go I guess.' I said. Fiona laughed too.

'Lets go dance again.' she made her way to the middle of the dance floor and we all followed and got back in our circle formation again and danced together, not letting anyone else into our group. It was so hot in here, so many bodies in a tight space.

After a while I needed a drink so I made hand gestures to show I was going to the bar, this time I got everyone a drink and a bottle of water each. As I tried to make my way to our table carrying our tray people were pushing towards the bar and bumping into me making it difficult to balance the drinks. Lucas appeared out of nowhere and took the tray from me and balanced it on one hand and looped his other arm through mine and lead me back to our table.

'Thanks.' I said when we got back to our table. I lifted my glass of prosecco and took a sip, I wasn't planning on going anywhere just yet so there was no rush to get it, besides, I was way more than tipsy right now, so it wasn't a bad idea to slow down a bit.

'Are you alright? You seem a bit unsteady on your feet.' Lucas asked.

'I'm fine, I'm just enjoying myself, you need to relax Lucas.' I said looking behind him where there were two lines forming, to see what it was for. 'Ooh look, uv face paint, come with me.' I wandered off taking my glass of prosecco with me and got in line. Lucas wasn't far behind.

15 minutes later I had green, blue and pink swirls on either side of my face framing my eyes and I'd managed to talk Lucas into getting war paint lines painted on his too. We walked back to our table and I handed him his drink as I took another swig of my prosecco, managing to spill a little down the front of my dress. Lucas lifted a napkin from the table and started dabbing my dress and I burst out laughing. 'What are you laughing at?' he asked clearly confused.

'You're like my mother. Stop. Lets get a photo with our faces painted like this.'

He mumbled something under his breath but came to stand beside me and put his arm around me. My whole body jerked at his touch and I fumbled with my selfie camera until he laughed and took my phone off me and and held it up and took our photo. Then instead of giving me my phone back, he opened my phone book and dialled a number. 'Hey, what are you doing?' I asked.
'I realised this morning that I don't have your phone number, so I've saved my number and rang myself from your phone. I wanted to wish you a Happy Birthday this morning and I've just realised I still haven't. Happy Birthday Ashton.' he turned and wrapped his other arm around my waist sending tingles down my spine and gave me a light kiss on my cheek, but he didn't move away and I didn't want him to. I looked up at him, his intense gaze fixed on mine, sure he was going to kiss me for real this time. When someone bumped into his back and pushed me back into the table wobbling all the drinks, but thankfully not knocking them over. I looked over his shoulder and seen Adam and Fiona nearly upon us, Adam looking at us and our close proximity to eachother with a hurt look in

THE DRUIDS OF BUSHMILLS - BOOK 1 - THE AWAKENING

his eyes. I side stepped out of Lucas's hold and nearly lost my balance and toppled sideways only Lucas put his hand out quick as lightening to stop me from falling and pulling me to him bringing us closer yet again just in time for Adam and Fiona to reach our table.' I looked up alarmed and Fiona saved me by speaking, 'Hey where did you's get to? Oh look you got your faces painted. I love it. Here Adam.' She passed him his drink and he downed it in one go, looking angry. She picked up her own drink and took a sip.

'It's getting late, I think we should get out of here.' he said.

'Yes I think it would be a good idea to get Ashton home, she's a bit unsteady on her feet, I just had to catch her to stop her from falling.' He laughed. I was sure he was trying to make light of the situation, as he had picked up on the weird vibe from Adam.

'Nooo, I don't want to go home yet.' Fiona whined.

'You need to go home too.' Lucas said in a tone that brokered no argument.

'Fine, but at least let me finish my drink. Honestly you would think you were my Dad, you're only a few minutes older than me.' she huffed.

I laughed, 'I just said to him a few minutes ago he was acting like my Mum.'

'He needs to chill out.' Fiona said, rolling her eyes at him. She was hilarious when she was drunk.

'I'll call a taxi.' Lucas said, taking his phone from his pocket and trying to find somewhere quieter to make the call, plugging one ear with his finger, as if that would help block out the noise in here. I watched him shouting over the music. Eventually he came back and told us our taxi would be there in a few minutes. Everyone finished there drinks up, Adam didn't seem to have much to say as we made our way outside and waited for our taxi to come.

'I have had theeeee best night, we have to come back here again soon.' Fiona said.

'Me too, thanks for planning this. I've had a great birthday.' I said.

Our taxi came a few minutes later, just on time because I was starting to get cold, summer or not. Adam got in the front on his own and didn't say a word. Fiona, Lucas and I got in the back, I was in the middle between Fiona and Lucas. It was around a 20 minute drive back to Granny's. Fiona after taking a fit of the giggles, promptly fell asleep. 'I think it might be better to bring her into my house and put her in one of the spare bedrooms when we get back. You guys can stay too.' I said.

'Thanks, as long as your Granny doesn't mind.' Lucas said. I looked up to see Adam glaring at me in the rearview mirror but he still didn't say a word. Seriously this was getting awkward. This was the last thing I wanted or needed. I decided to just shut up then I couldn't say or do anything else to piss anyone off.

When we arrived at Granny's house I woke Fiona up. Adam paid the taxi driver and then went around and opened her door and helped her out. She was even more unsteady on her feet than I was. Adam gave up trying to help her walk and just lifted her and put her over his shoulder, she laughed and shouted, 'For god's sake Adam, put me down, I can walk.'

'Well then you should have done a better a job of it.' he grumbled good humouredly, seeming to have snapped out of his mood a bit.

Lucas and I followed them into the house. Adam abandoned Fiona at the bottom of the stairs like a sack of potatoes and walked into the kitchen, no doubt to raid the fridge for left overs. He really did love his food.

I tried to pull Fiona up with both my hands pulling her arm, but instead of me pulling her to her feet, she pulled me to the floor beside her. We both started to laugh, we tried to get up but we just laughed more. Lucas looked at the two of us as if we were nuts but he couldn't help but join in the laughter. He came and pulled us both up one by one. He helped Fiona first and then he pulled me up by both hands so hard that my chest bumped into his and I nearly fell over again. He put his hands around my waist to steady me, what was not steady was my heartbeat, it was galloping out of my chest. I looked up at him.

'Oh my God, you two just can't help yourselves, get a room.' Fiona said and turned and walked into the kitchen after Adam. I looked after her gobsmacked. My could feel the blood travelling up my neck to my face. I looked down and tried to turn out of Lucas's grip and walk after her but he held me in place and fixed me with a look so intense that I couldn't look away. I momentarily forgot my embarassment and stared back at him, taking in his tanned skin, his long eyelashes any girl would envy, the freckle beside his eye, his sharp jaw line. Without saying a word, he slid his hands down my waist, past the curve of my ass, down my legs over my dress until he reached bare skin and I gasped, then so quickly I didn't know what was happening, he put one arm under my legs and the other under my arm and picked me up and began to walk up the stairs. As he did one of my shoes fell off. I protested, 'What are you doing?'

'Getting a room.' he said with a grin.

He took me upstairs to my room, managing to open my bedroom

door whilst holding my weight. He stepped through the door and then closed it with his back and walked over and laid me gently down on the bed, he took my other shoe off caressing the bottom of my foot on the way past making me shiver. He bent down over me and I sucked in a breath in expectation of the kiss that was about to come and instead he ducked his head and placed a soft kiss on my collar bone, so gentle that it made my skin tingle, then another at the corner of my mouth and then he whispered, 'Good night Ashton, happy birthday.' He turned and began to walk away, but before he got very far I couldn't hold myself back from saying 'What the fuck Lucas?'

He froze with his back to me. Then slowly turned around, a look of utter bewilderment on his face.

I sat upright and glared at him.

'What's wrong?' he asked.

'Are you joking? What is with all the mixed signals and teasing? Don't you want to kiss me?' I asked furiously.

'Yes, of course I want to kiss you. I just didn't want to take advantage of you when you were drunk.' he said carefully.

'Well then let me ask you this, are you drunk right now?'

'I guess a little. Why?' he asked confused.

'So if I were to kiss you right now whilst you're drunk that would be considered taking advantage of you? Or is that just some sexist notion you have that only counts when a woman is drunk?'

He released a breath and laughed, he laughed so hard his face turned scarlet and I wondered had he forgot to breathe.

I was so furious I didn't want to laugh, but seeing how much he was cracking up I couldn't help but laugh too. When he had calmed down, he came over and sat on the edge of my bed and pushed my hair back out of my face. I turned my head the other way, to make it clear that even if he wanted to kiss me, that I no longer wanted to kiss him. I was still angry.

He grabbed me roughly by the chin and turned my face so I had to look him in the eye. 'I'm sorry I didn't mean to tease you or to be sexist. I seem to be doing everything wrong, but it's only because I like you so much. I want us to get to know eachother. There just hasn't been a lot of time for that with everything going on. I want to kiss you so much all the time that I have to stop myself. How would you like to spend some time together tomorrow? We could go to the Giant's Causeway.'

'I can't tomorrow. I promised Mia that we would meet up.'

'Oh yeah I forgot about that, I was going to join you if that's alright?'

'I suppose so.'

He grinned at me.

'I'm going to go and let you get some sleep, but I will see you in the morning.' he said.

'Who said I wanted to go to sleep? You just brought me up here and put me to bed like a child.' I said sulkily.

He laughed again. 'Ok fair enough. I apologise. If you don't want to go to sleep what do you want to do?' he asked.

'Well first of all I want to get this dress off. Give me a minute.'

I went to my wardrobe and grabbed a pair of shorts and t-shirt pajamas and then went into the ensuite to get changed. When I came back into the room Lucas had made himself comfortable on my bed, he'd taken his shoes off and was lying back with his arms behind his head on my pillows.

'I've decided what I want to do.' I announced standing beside the bed.

'What's that then?' Lucas asked.

'Let's go see if Granny has anymore drink and we can get Adam and Fiona on the way and go to the games room.'

'More drink?' he raised his eyebrows at me.

'It's my birthday.' was all I said.

'Sounds like a plan.' he said bouncing to his feet.

We went downstairs and into the kitchen but Fiona and Adam were nowhere to be seen.

'I wonder where they've gone.' I said.

'They were both drunk, my guess is to bed.' Adam replied.

I opened the fridge and lifted out a bottle of prosecco, then walked to Granny's drink trolley that looked a globe and opened the top. 'What do you want? There's beer, wine, prosecco, gin, whiskey and vodka.'

'I'll just share your prosecco.' he said getting two glasses and setting them on the table. I opened the prosecco and poured us both a glass and then noticed movement out of the corner of my eye in the sunroom. I turned around and there was Fiona knees straddled either side of Adam, her dress riding up her thighs, in one of the grey leather armchairs, kissing him like there was no tomorrow. Adam was holding her to him by the elbows. I reeled in shock. Only a few hours ago Adam told me he liked me and sweetly asked me to consider him, now he was busy snogging the face off what I was hoping was going to be my new best friend. Lucas must have noticed me staring.

'What the fuck?' he said storming to the sunroom, opening the door and barking out 'Fiona what the hell are you doing? Get off him.'

Fiona and Adam both looked up in shock, she quickly got up and pulled her dress down to protect her modesty.

'You're drunk, I think you need to go to bed.' he said furiously. Fiona walked out of the room unsteadily without saying another word.

Lucas rounded on Adam, 'What are you doing man? Can't you see how drunk she is, could you just not keep your hands to yourself?'

Adam looked up at me bleary eyed, it was then I noticed the half drank bottle of whiskey on the table and the two shot glasses. How much could they have drank in the short time that we were away?

'Ashton, I'm sorry.' he said.

Lucas looked from Adam to me, clearly baffled about why Adam was apologising to me. Then it was clear the penny dropped.

'Get the fuck out of my sight.' Lucas growled.

Adam looked back at him in disgust, but he didn't say a word, he just got up and instead of going upstairs to bed, he went through the kitchen and out the back door. The motion sensor lights came on out the back so I could see him storming off in the direction of the outhouses.

I finally found my voice, 'Where the hell is he going?'

'It's ok, he's probably just going home, his house isn't far from here. Is there something going on with you and Adam?' he asked clenching his jaw

'Woah where did that come from?' I asked

'I seen the way that he looked at you and why else would he apologise?'

'No there is nothing going on with me and Adam. Why would you even care if there was?' I said getting annoyed at his attitude with me.

'Because if he has something going on with you then he was just leading my sister on and also I wouldn't like it if he treated you like that.' he softened slightly. 'I know he has feelings for you Ashton, I just don't want him using my sister as a way to get over you.'

I walked over to the table and lifted my prosecco and took a long drink and then sat down.

'Do you have feelings for him?' he asked.

'Honestly? I don't know. You know he asked me the same thing about you earlier tonight.'

'And what did you say.'

'I said I don't know.'

'Right then, great.' He walked over and picked up his glass and downed it one. Then he stood just in front of me and held out his hand. I looked at him bewildered but I placed my hand in his and he pulled me to my feet. There was no preamble, he didn't utter a word, still holding my hand he wrapped his other arm around me and kissed me hard and long and slow and the electricity I felt every time I seen or touched him intensified to a new level until I felt like it was going to explode from my skin, I kissed him back with the same intensity, tasting the prosecco on his lips and drinking it in until I couldn't get enough. He traced his fingers along my collar bone and it undid me, I ran my hands over his shoulders, down his torso and then the electricity I was feeling literally came to life as I felt a shock through my hand, he yelled and jumped back, there was a smoking hole in his t-shirt. He laughed, I looked at him in shock, and he laughed more at the look on my face, I couldn't help but laugh too. 'I'm so sorry I didn't mean to.' I said embarassed.

'It's ok it was just an accident.' he said still smiling. I couldn't wipe the silly smile of my face either, despite just nearly burning a hole through Lucas's torso.

'Are you hurt?' I asked.

'No it just stings a little but I'm fine.' he said, I had a feeling he was putting a brave face on it.

'Let me look,' I said as I approached him to peer through the hole in his t-shirt, the skin looked really red. 'Take your t-shirt off.' He raised his eyebrows at me still smiling but did as he was told. He pulled his t-shirt over his head and then let it dangle from his hand. I couldn't help but stare, he was beautiful with his golden tan, muscled torso and bright red burn, shoot me now. 'That looks sore, sit down, I'll be back in a second.' I went to the bathroom beside the games room and got a clean flannel and a bowl of tepid water and brought it to him. I held it to the wound, he hissed when it made contact with his skin but quickly recovered his manly calm.

'Are you ok?' I asked. 'I'm really sorry, I don't know how that happened.'

'I'm fine Ashton, stop apologising, it was an accident, I'll be ok. Can I ask you something though?'

'You just did.' I said.

'You're hilarious.' he said dryly.

'Sure, go for it, since I just tried to electrocute you, but then we're even.' he laughed.

'Are you still not sure if you like me?' he grinned.

I batted at his arm, then remembered he was injured, so instead I replied, 'I don't know, I need more information before I can make an informed decision on that.' I said haughtily, then broke into a smile.

'Fine what do you need to know, we're going to be here for a while tending to my near fatal injury so I guess I have time.'

'Thanks for the guilt trip I said. I don't know, tell me everything. Do you want another drink?'

'Yeah sure, it might help with the pain.' he grinned again.

'Oh give over would you, I think you'll live.' I lifted my glass of prosecco and downed the rest, I needed it after that traumatic experience, then I lifted the bottle and poured us both another glass and handed his to him.

'You know what would be cool,' I said having a thought. 'If I knew how to use my necromancer abilities to heal, then I wouldn't have to listen to you whine about that tiny burn.'

He laughed again. 'Well why couldn't you do it? It's just like using your other magic and you seem to have no problem with that.'

'When I was using my magic earlier, I could only see 4 strands, green for earth, blue for water, red for fire and white for air.'

'You can see your magic?' he asked clearly surprised.

'Can't you? Is that not a thing? I just thought that was normal.'

'I've never heard of anyone else seeing their own magic. But then I've never heard of anyone else with 5 types of magic. Look and see if you can find another strand.'

'Maybe it's just my overactive imagination. Ok I'll try.'

I closed my eyes and concentrated on that place in my belly were my magic came from, I could see the red, white, green and blue strands, I pushed past them all and found what I was looking for, it was more difficult to see because it was black and the other strands were hiding it. Now I pulled on it and pushed it up through my body and over my shoulders and down through my arms then I opened my eyes, 'I've got it.' I stepped forward and pushed Lucas's hand out of the way and pressed the palm of my hand against his now blistering burn and pushed the magic out through my hand and into the wound. Lucas's whole body jolted and he slumped over falling forward to the ground whilst I tried to catch him and cushion his fall, but he was too big and heavy and fell face first into my shoulder, knocking me sprawling onto my back. 'Oh my God, Lucas are you ok?'

'I'm fine I think, but how did I get here?' The voice came from behind me. I looked back and screamed. I scrambled backwards away from Lucas's body and got to my feet and then turned to look at the transparent figure standing before me, Lucas was a ghost. 'Oh my God I did this I killed you, I'm so sorry, how do I fix this?' I panicked.

Lucas looked back at me in shock and then it was a like a light bulb was switched on. 'Oh. That's my body.'

'What have I done, what have I done, what have I done.' I rambled over and over again, distraught at what I had done.

'It's ok Ashton, just calm down and think. You must have pulled my soul from my body, so you should be able to just shove it back in there.' he said questioningly.

'Erm yeah I guess, but I didn't feel like I was pulling from you, I was pulling from my magic and pushing it into your burn.'

'Maybe you accidentally pulled from me whilst trying to pull on your magic.' he said.

'Yeah that makes sense. But I don't know how to pull your soul back into your body. How can I use my magic on you if you're a spirit. Couldn't you just try and enter your body again?' I asked hopefully.
'I can try but if magic pulled me out I would think magic will have to put me back in otherwise every single person that ever died would just try to re-enter their body in their spirit form.' he said uncertainly.

'Oh god this is literally a nightmare. I'm so sorry Lucas.' I panicked again.

'Calm down Ashton, I could be wrong, let me try.' he said gliding towards his body in his spirit form and hovering face down above it and then his spirit form and his body merged but I could still see the outline of his spirit form so I knew already that it didn't work. He raised his head up out of his body in his spirit form and it was the creepiest thing I'd ever seen. I shivered. 'Didn't work.' he said.

'How are you so calm right now? I am freaking out. I killed you. I'm a murderer.'

He laughed. 'I have faith that you can fix this, that's why I am calm. Besides it feels cool to float.'

'Ok, no pressure then. Ok so if you stay inside your body, what am I even saying.' I mumbled to myself. I took a deep breath. 'Ok so if you stay inside your body, then I'll try and push my spirit magic into you to fix this mess.'

'Ok good plan, I'm ready.' Lucas said, I had a feeling he was enjoying this.

I approached Lucas's body and Lucas's ghost, I closed my eyes and found the black strand of my spirit magic, I opened them and knelt down beside Lucas's body and pressed the palm of my hand to his back. Nothing happened. Then I thought of something. I had done something similar when I was a child, when I brought back the mouse, so I was definitely capable of bringing a living thing back to life, I just had to figure out a way to make his spirit rejoin his body. Then it hit me, I had to restart his heart. I didn't need to be touching him either. I let my hand hover over where his heart would be and pushed my magic out, I felt it flow into his heart and wrap around it massaging it as if I was giving him magical cpr. His spirit had disappeared but I couldn't tell if he was breathing. I rolled him on to his back and pushed more of my magic into his heart, I was getting dizzy, but I couldn't stop. I held my hand in place and bent down and tilted back his head and breathed into his mouth as I massaged his heart with my magic, it wasn't working and I was getting more and more light headed. I closed my eyes having an idea, I pulled on the strand of white air magic and held out my left hand and pushed the air magic into his mouth as I used the spirit magic on his heart with my right hand, I was on the verge of passing out when Lucas took a gasping breath and opened his eyes. That was the last thing I seen before I passed out.

Chapter 14

I woke up, well I thought I was awake, everything was foggy, my eyes were so heavy, too heavy to open, my head pounded, maybe I should just go back to sleep, yeah that's a good idea.

'I think she's awake.' I heard a voice faraway in the background. I recognised it, but I couldn't remember who it belonged to.

'Maybe we should let her sleep a while longer. She will be exhausted from using so much powerful magic.'

'We must wake her and get her to drink this. It's the only thing that will help. Help me sit her up.' I knew that voice too but everything was too foggy.

I felt arms around me, pulling me up, but my body was floppy, I didn't have any control over myself. Then something was pressed against my lips opening them and a cool foul tasting liquid entered my mouth, I gulped unintentionally and swallowed. I shot upright in bed fully alert now. My mum, Lucas and Granny were here, Lucas was holding me up, my Granny was holding a cup that I'd nearly knocked out of her hand, my Mum was watching carefully.

'What's wrong, why are you all here?' I asked.

'Do you remember what happened last night?' Mum asked.

I thought back to last night in Halo, I must have had way too much to drink. 'Here take another drink of this.' Granny held the cup out to me, I looked at it in disgust. 'Drink it or I'll make you' she warned. I hastily took the cup from her hands and took another drink. I instantly became more alert, then it hit me. I covered my mouth with my free hand. 'Oh my god I killed Lucas last night.'

'Oh for goodness sake, don't be so dramatic Ashton, he's not dead he's standing right here.' At that moment I realised that he was still holding onto me, not because I needed his help anymore, but it seemed as though he didn't want to let go. He looked worried. I sat completely upright.

'I fixed it.' I said in relief.

'Yes you fixed it, and completely drained your own magic in the process. You need to start smaller than resurrection Ashton. You will worry everyone if you keep passing out like this all the time.' Granny scolded.

'I'm sorry, I didn't mean to, I was trying to heal a burn I gave Lucas.' I said.

'How in the name of God did you burn him.' Mum asked as the memory came back to me and my face went purple. Granny chuckled, Mum just glared, Lucas smirked.

'How do you feel?' Granny asked.

'Hungover. Head hurts.' I grumbled.

'That'll be from overusing your magic. You need to be careful Ashton. There are dangers with using so much magic at once, if you drain yourself too much you can die.' Granny said.

'Why did no one tell me this sooner, I would have been more careful.' I asked.

'Because it's something that hasn't happened for a very long time. But you are unusually powerful, even more so because you have 5 types of magic. So it's best to be cautious, you will eventually learn your limits.'

'Well I'm glad in this case I didn't know my limits because other wise Lucas might have died.' I said grouchily.

'You need to finish that.' Mum pointed towards the cup.
'Why does it have to be so disgusting.' I moaned.

'Just drink.' Mum ordered.

I drank the rest of the disgusting contents of the cup. As bad as it was, it worked. I felt much more human by the time I finished it.

'What time is it?' I asked looking around for my phone but not finding it.

'It's just after 11.30 am.' Lucas said looking at his watch. 'Why what's wrong?'

'I'm supposed to be meeting with Mia today.'

'Oh, I didn't realise you were friendly with Mia.' Granny said.

'Well actually, we're not really all that friendly, I don't think she likes me very much, but I want to help her. We're going to try and gather support for Sophia, so that David will agree to help us free her from the necromancers.'

'Ashton you can't do this.' my Mum said incredulous.

'Ashton, David won't agree to this. He can't be seen to be making an exception for his own Grand daughter. He will be accused of being a traitor and lose all respect of our Grove.'

'Are you kidding? So being High Priest of the Grove comes before family?' I fumed.

'It's not like that Ashton.' Granny said sadly.

'Well then what's it like?' I said my voice raising.

'He cannot be SEEN, to be making an exception.' The penny dropped. I nodded back. My Mum turned to look at Granny in disbelief. Lucas smiled. In that moment my mind was made up about what we had to do.

'Right, well I'm going to get showered if I could have some privacy please.' I said.

'I'll go make you some tea and something to eat, you need to get your energy up. Take it easy.' Granny said.

'Ashton, I don't know what you're planning, but you need to stop, I won't let you put yourself in danger.'

'I'm already in danger Mum. Either help me or stay out of it.' I snapped back. She stormed out of the room, with Granny leaving after her.

Lucas lingered behind. 'Are you sure you're feeling alright?' he asked.

'Yeah I'm fine, a little shaky, but my headache has mostly gone away, I'm sure I'll be fine after something to eat.'

'What you did last night was amazing. I knew you could do it. I've never seen anyone use two types of magic together like that.'

'Well that's not surprising considering I'm the only one with two types of magic.' I said.

'That's not true.' he replied.

'What do you mean it's not true? All I've heard about since I've got here is how I'm the only one with more than one type of magic.' I said confused.

'No, you're the only one with five types of magic. There are some people who have two. I've even heard of people with three.'

'Oh, I thought I was special.' I said good humouredly.

'You are special.' he looked at me with that intense look again.

'So who are these other people with two types of magic. Do we know any of them?'

'You're looking at one of them.' he said then held his breath awaiting my reaction.

'You're joking. How could you not tell me this before now?' I asked.

'It just never came up.' he said sheepishly. I threw my pillow at him. He held his hands up in surrender. 'I'm sorry.'

'Is there anyone else that I know?' I asked.

'Fiona.' he whispered.

I was incredulous. 'I can't believe you would keep this from me. Who else?' I ordered.

'Some secrets aren't mine to tell.'

'What the hell does that mean?'

'Look Ashton, you don't understand. Before you came along, it was considered unusual to have more than one type of magic. People don't trust what they don't know, so most people with more than one type of magic like to keep it to themselves.'

'So does no one else know that you have more than one type of magic?' I asked.

'Just David, your Granny, my Mum and now you.'

'But how is that possible? Surely people could tell from the signs from your ancestors at your ceremony.'

'Fiona and I had a private ceremony.'

'I didn't know we could do that. I would have preferred a private ceremony. Instead of all those people I didn't know staring at me and making me nervous.'

'Fiona and I travelled for a year, people just assume that we had our ceremony with another Grove whilst we were away.'

'So what type of magic do you have?' I asked.

'Fire and water.' he said lifting a hand and turning it palm up and a flame erupting from it then he doused the flame with water from his other hand.

'That's weird isn't it, to have pretty much opposite types of magic.' I said.

'You have opposite types of magic.' he said smiling.

'Fair point.' I conceded. 'Well I'm going to get a shower now.'

'Ok I'll leave you to it.' he said but still lingered.

'This is the part where you turn and leave.' I said sarcastically.

He laughed and approached me where I was sitting on the bed, 'I just wanted to do this.' He bent down and kissed me, long and slow and gentle, compared to our kiss last night. I could feel the electricity sparking again and pushed it down to avoid any unwanted side affects. I forgot all about getting a shower and sank into the kiss. He broke away, leaving me wanting more.

'I'll wait for you downstairs.' He kissed my nose and got up to leave when I called him back, 'Lucas, I won't tell anyone the secret about your magic'.

'I know.' was all he said and he smiled as he left the room.

I got up and looked for my phone but I couldn't find it anywhere. I maybe left it downstairs last night. I showered quickly and dressed and went downstairs.

Mum, Granny, Fiona, Lucas, and Leona were sitting around the table eating. 'Good afternoon.' Mum said smiling. Fiona looked a little sick sitting in the corner, she didn't look up as I came in, Lucas locked eyes with me and I felt a jolt of electricity. Granny got up to get me a plate and handed me a bacon bap and a cup of tea. 'Thanks Granny.' I sat down.

'Good night last night?' Leona asked smiling.

'Yeah something like that.' I smiled back.

'I guessed as much, Adam came in like a herd of elephants last night, he was banging about trying to make something to eat and then passed out on top of his bed with all his clothes on and left me to clean up his mess. He's still nursing his hangover in bed.'

I glanced at Fiona, her face was going an alarming shade of red. I smiled.

'I think we were all a bit worse for wear this morning.' I said.

'So, what's your plans for today?'she asked.

'Just going to see a friend.' I said.

Mum glared at me. Leona, clearly not in the loop said, 'That's great you're making friends already.'

'Yip' I said, 'You guys are coming too aren't you?' I asked Fiona and Lucas.

Fiona just nodded, 'Yeah we're coming.' Lucas said.

I ate my bacon sandwich and drank my tea, feeling much more human now. 'Has anyone seen my phone? I must have left it down here somewhere last night.'

'Your handbag is here dear, maybe its inside.' Granny said getting up and retrieving my handbag from where it was hanging in the utility room. 'I found it this morning and hung it up for you.'

'Thanks Granny,' I said as she handed it to me and I opened it, finding my phone inside with the battery completely depleted. 'I'm just going to charge this.'

I left and went back to my room and put my phone on the charger. I lay on my bed whilst I waited for my phone to charge. My door knocked. 'Come in,' I called.

It was Fiona, she came over and sat on the armchair beside my bed.

'How are you feeling?' she asked.

'I'm ok now, I feel much better. How are you doing today? You look a little fragile.'

'I feel awful, I'm so sorry Ashton. I was so drunk last night, I should never have kissed Adam. It was all me, he was trying to shove me off him when you and Lucas came in.'
'Hey, it's ok, it's not up to me who Adam kisses, or who you kiss. I was just surprised I guess after what Adam said to me last night. Besides Lucas and I kind of kissed last night. And this morning actually.'

Fiona visibly brightened. 'Thank you for being so understanding. I wasn't sure how you felt about Adam, but I know it's you that he likes so I don't know what I was thinking.'

'Really it's fine don't worry, Adam and I are just friends.'

'So what's the plan for today?'

'We're going to see Mia, I'm going to text her when my phone's charged. Granny said that David can't be seen supporting us, so we are on our own. We can't involve David, so we will have to break Sophia out on our own.'

'Alot of people aren't going to go against the High Priest. That's going to limit who we can ask for help.' Fiona said thoughtfully.

'It's ok, we need to get Adam on board, I can ask my cousins to help, then Mia can ask her and Sophia's friends.'

'I know a couple of people we can ask too.' Fiona said.

'Brilliant, I'm going to text Mia now.'

I sent Mia a text message asking her where and when she wanted to meet. Around 10 minutes later my phone beeped in response.

Meet me at Bushfoot Strand at 2pm

I let my phone charge a little longer and text my cousins Jacob, Anna and Caitlyn. Caitlyn couldn't make it, but Jacob and Anna were going to meet us at Bushfoot Strand.

We went downstairs and got Lucas and grabbed some drinks and snacks a picnic blanket. We got in my car and Fiona directed me to Adam's house. It really was close to my house, I could have walked there in two minutes. I got out of my Range Rover and knocked the door loudly. There was no answer, so I tried again.

I could hear movement so I banged the door this time. 'Adam answer the door, hurry up we need to go.'

Finally he came and answered the door, he looked a lot fresher than I expected. 'Hey' he said when he opened the door.

'We need to go Adam, we're going to Bushfoot Strand to meet Mia, we have to be there for 2pm so get ready and come on.'

'Ok I'll come but I'm not coming for Sophia, I'm coming to make sure you stay out of trouble. I wanted to talk to you Ashton. Last night wasn't what it looked like.'

'You don't need to explain yourself Adam, first of all Fiona has already explained what happened, secondly it's none of my business who you kiss.' I don't know why, but I couldn't help but be a little snarky with him. Fiona had explained what had happened and I kissed Lucas anyway, so I had no right to be annoyed.

'Ok then, give me a minute.'

I went back to the car and waited with Fiona and Lucas. Adam came out a few minutes later and got in the back with Lucas.

'Sorry about last night bro. I got the wrong impression.' Lucas said to Adam.

'No worries, drink in wits out.' Adam said and laughed.

Lucas laughed in response and just like that their little tiff was over.

It took us just under 10 minutes to get to Bushfoot Strand. I noticed Mia parked in her Ford Focus not far from us and went over to talk to her. When she seen me she put the electric window down. 'Hi Ashton, thanks for coming. Should we go on down to the beach and wait for everyone. There's more people here than I expected today and I don't want to be over heard.'

I went back to my car and everyone else filed out and helped me get our snacks and picnic blanket. We just looked like anyone else going to the beach. Mia met us on the walk down, she was with 3 other girls and a guy. 'We have some more people coming.' she said. 'This is Courtney, Emily, Leanne and Michael.' she pointed each of them out.

'Hi,' I waved. 'My cousins Jacob and Anna are coming too. Lucas, Adam and Fiona have reached out to a few people too.'

When we reached the beach we walked around the strand to a more private area and laid out our blankets. Jacob and Anna arrived soon after we did, as did Mia's friends, Shannon, Ryan, Liam, Diane and Macie. I recognised a few of them from the last time we were here.

We sat around chatting and eating while waiting on the latecomers arriving.

I walked over and sat beside Mia. 'I need to talk to you privately.' She got up and followed me over to some large rocks and we sat on them. 'So my Granny said your Granda David can't be seen to help us, as people will think he's using his position as High Priest to give preferential treatment to his family. So we're on our own with this, but I think if we have the numbers, we should act and ask for forgiveness later. They're not going to turn Sophia back over to the necromancers once we save her. We could even say she came back of her own free will. What do you think?'

'I think that could actually work. Well if we have the numbers and if we can put a plan together of how we're going to get into the ruins to save her. I think we need more info to find out where she is actually being held, that is if she is being held at all. I've been thinking about this a lot and I might have to accept the possibility that she won't want to come back.'

'You know your sister better than anyone Mia. Do you really think she will want to stay with the necromancers?' I asked.

'No, but then I never thought she would betray us in the first place.'

'Ok, well lets wait and see who actually comes and we can take it from there.'

We walked back over to our picnic blankets and sat down. It had turned out to be a lovely day, if a little windy, but it was always windy this close to the sea. I sat and enjoyed the sunshine whilst we waited.

I closed my eyes to enjoy the sunshine. I heard a voice calling my name in the distance and opened my eyes. I could see a figure waving from far away, it couldn't be. It looked like Granny, carrying a picnic basket and with her it looked like Auntie Emma, Uncle Mark, Uncle Malcolm, Leona and was that my Mum? I stood up and waved. As they got closer I could see that I was right, my Mum had came, even though she had protested, she still came.

When they got closer my Uncle Malcolm and Uncle Mark unfolded the chairs they'd brought with them and Granny laid out a blanket with a whole picnic with everything from crackers and cheese and sandwiches to fruit and biscuits.

I got up and went to where my Mum was sitting. 'I can't believe you came. How did you know where we were?' I asked.

'You guys aren't as sneaky as you think. Granny's sneakier, there's a tracker on your Range Rover. Once we knew your location we packed up a picnic and followed you down here.'

I laughed. Why did that not surprise me. 'Well I'm glad you came, thank you.' I said.

'I only came to keep you out of trouble.' she grumbled and I grinned at her.

'Adam said the same thing.'

'He's got sense, I like him.' she smiled.

Ten more people arrived, Lucas's friends Daniel, William and Thomas with his girlfriend Lisa, Adam's friends Lyndsey , Rhianne and Amy, why did it not surprise me they were all girls. Then Fiona's friends Andy, Graham and Michelle. At my count there were 32 of us. We might actually be able to make this work.

I went and spoke to Mia. 'Has everyone arrived that you were waiting on? We have more people here than I expected.'

'Don't sound so surprised. Yeah I think this is pretty much it.'

'I'm just glad we have this much support, it will hopefully make our job a lot easier. Are you going to speak to everyone now?'

'Yeah I guess so.' she said getting up and walking to the highest point on the sand so everyone could see her.

'Hi everyone,' she shouted above the chattering going on around her. All but a few people settled down and turned to look at her, the ones that continued talking were soon shushed and turned to attention. 'Thank you all for coming today, I appreciate it. As you all know my sister Sophia has been seeing a necromancer, and has naively betrayed Ashton to them. I know what she has done is a huge betrayal, so much so my own Mother and Grandad have turned their backs on her. But I'm here to ask you all to find it within yourselves to forgive her or if you can't forgive her, at least have enough empathy to not leave her to her fate with the necromancers. My sister has previously been of good character and I believe she has been mislead by this necromancer. Ashton herself approached me and asked me could she help, so if she can find it within her to care enough to help my sister then hopefully you all can too. Our plan is to rescue her from the Dunluce Castle ruins, the necromancers base, as this is the only place we think they could be holding her. So we will need numbers and it may be dangerous, but the more of us there are, the more likely we are to be successful. I am scared for my sister and what the necromancers might be doing to her. If you don't want to help, leave now and we won't hold it against you. If you do want to help, we need a plan, so any knowledge of the ruins will be helpful. Thank you.'

Granny stood up, 'On behalf of myself and my family, I want you to know that we will all help and do whatever it takes to help get Sophia back.'

Lucas's friends Thomas and Lisa got up and left, but everyone else there stood and said they would help. I was glad we kept so many of our numbers. Thirty was a good number.

'Ok, thank you all for staying and agreeing to help. Now we need to come up with a plan. Does anyone have any inside knowledge of the ruins? Or entrances we can use to surprise them or avoid early detection? I am anxious to get to Sophia sooner rather than later, I already fear that she has been left with the necromancers for too long.' Mia spoke again.

Michael spoke up 'I'm not sure the ruins are our best bet. I know the necromancers have a base of sorts there, but it's only for show. They all have home's. Its only the lower ranks that hang out there. What if they've taken her somewhere else? I heard that one of their leaders recently bought the Marine Hotel in Ballycastle. It's kind of perfect, who would expect the necromancers to be hanging out in such a nice place.'

'How do you know this?' I asked.

'My cousin is an estate agent and she told me that it had been bought by necromancers.'

'No way I love that place.' Fiona said. Mia glared at her.

'How are we going to know where they're keeping Sophia, unless we actually see her with our own eyes. She could be at Dunluce Castle or the Marine Hotel, or her boyfriend John's house. As soon as the necromancers see us hanging around they're going to know what we're up to.' I thought out loud.

'I've thought about this. If we could just track Sophia's phone we would be able to find out where she is. That's if its still switched on. If not it might show us her last known location. The only problem is I have tried and I don't know her password.' Mia said.

'I might be able to help with that.' to my shock it was Granny who spoke.

'Have you been doing a lot of phone hacking lately Granny.' I said. Adam roared with laughter. There were a few other snickers.

'I know a guy.' was all she said in response and winked at me. 'Just get me her phone number and email address. I will hopefully have the details by the end of the day.'

Mia raised her eyebrows. 'Ok well I guess there's not much else we can do until we find out where she actually is. I'll give you the details.'

Everyone started to disperse after that agreeing to meet tonight or tomorrow, as soon as Granny had details of Sophia's location.

'Thanks for everything.' Mia said as we walked back to our cars. 'I hope this works out and we find out where she is or we will be going in blind.'

'Hopefully we won't be waiting too long until we find out for sure either way. I'll be in touch as soon as possible. Unless you want to come back to Granny's house and wait with us?' I asked.

'Would you mind? I don't want to impose. I just don't think I'll rest until I know where she is. I have barely slept in a week.'

'Of course. Come back with us. Bring your friends you came with too if you want.' I said.

'Thanks, I really appreciate this.'

'You don't need to keep thanking me Mia. Anyway I owe you, you saved me that night at Dunluce Castle.'

'Well my sister did try to get you kidnapped. I kind of felt like it would be rude to let you get yourself killed. Even if you were completely reckless.' she laughed.

'Fair enough.' I said.

CHAPTER 15

We all gathered back at Granny's house, well the family, plus Adam and his Mum, Fiona and Lucas and Mia and her friends Courtney, Emily, Leanne and Michael.

Granny got in touch with her contact as soon as we returned, so we were all just hanging around waiting for a response.

Granny made everyone something to eat whilst we waited. I was getting impatient.

'Hey, I whispered to Adam who was sitting beside me. 'Grab Fiona and Lucas and meet me at the clearing out back.' He gave me a look as if to say what are you up to. But he turned and spoke quietly to Lucas and Fiona and then followed me to the clearing. I hoped to go unnoticed but Mia looked up and met my eyes as we exited through the back door.

When we got to the clearing, Fiona spoke first. 'What's up?'

'I've been thinking about this and even once we know where Sophia is, we can't just rush in there unprepared, it's likely to get people killed. So I think we should go now and take a look around the Marine Hotel and Dunluce Castle and figure out a way in and out of both. Hopefully they will have Sophia's location by the time we return.'

'Wow Ashton doesn't want to rush into something.' Adam joked.

Fiona laughed, which I found kind of irritating.

'It's a good idea in theory, but how are we going to do it without being seen.' asked Lucas.

'I've been thinking about this too and I think I know a way. That's why I wanted you all to come out here, it's a little crazy but hear me out.' I said.

'There she is.' Adam grinned, I rolled my eyes at him.

'So, Granny told me not all necromancers can see ghosts, but even if they can, they aren't going to expect that ghosts are spying on them. What if I use my spirit power to make you all spirits so as you can get a look around the necromancers headquarters without being detected. I don't think they would suspect anything.'

'That could actually work, that's a really clever idea. I've just got one problem with it. How do you know that you can do this? I'm not doubting you, but if you've never done it before, how do you know you can take our spirits from our bodies and successfully reattach them afterwards. It's a little risky, I like this body, I would like to stay attached to it.' Adam always found a way to lighten the moment.

'Actually, I have done it before. Just once though.' I looked at Lucas, 'I was thinking maybe we could have a practice run.'

Adam and Fiona looked between Lucas and I clearly confused. I suppose I better explain. 'Last night I accidentally pulled Lucas's soul from his body, but look it's all good, I put him back together good as new.' I said my voice getting more high pitched as I went along.

'How do you accidentally pull someone's soul from their body?' Adam asked incredulously

'I was trying to use my spirit power to heal Lucas, he got burnt.' I said, not wanting to explain how he had got burnt.

Adam's eyebrows hit his hairline. 'Ok so it's encouraging that you were able to reattach his soul to his body, but you've only done it once, are you sure you're up to doing this again, not just once but three times.'
'Ashton is leaving out there part where she passed out after doing it and only woke up this morning.' Lucas added.

'I don't know this seems a little reckless Ashton.' Fiona said, disapprovingly.

'Ok, ok. I get all of your points but I have an idea. Granny mixed this concoction for me and made me drink it and it made me almost as good as new. So I was thinking I could get her to make me some so that I can drink it to stop me from passing out.'

'That might work.' Lucas pondered.

'So is anyone up for trying now? A practice run?' I asked, 'I can ask Granny to prepare me some first.'

'Yeah that might be a good idea.' Adam said.

We went back inside and I asked Granny to come into the sunroom to talk to me. I was hoping she would take this well.

'Is everything alright dear?' she asked.

'Yes everything is great. I just have an idea and I need your help.'

'And what would your idea be?' she asked cautiously.

'So I was thinking, regardless of where Sophia is being held, we can't go in blind, it would be too dangerous. Then I remembered you saying that not all necromancers were powerful enough to see spirits. But even if they were, they wouldn't expect spirits to be spying on them. So I thought I could remove Adam, Lucas and Fiona's spirits from their bodies to allow them to spy on the necromancers and then find out exactly where Sophia is and how to get to her and then put their spirits back in like I done with Lucas last night. But then I would run into the obvious problem of passing out. So I thought if you made me some of your concoction before hand, we could practice before putting it to the test.'

'Oh Ashton, it's a good idea, but it's much too dangerous. There is no one here with enough knowledge of necromancer abilities to help guide you and I fear that you got lucky last night with Lucas. I think it's best that you don't try again.'

'There must be necromancers who can do this type of thing. Surely I'm not the first, so there must be a method of doing it. How am I going to figure out my necromancer abilities if I don't try to use them. I'm certain I can put the spirit back after pulling it out, but I'm just worried about having enough juice to do it multiple times. I would never suggest it if I didn't think I can do it.'

Granny nodded, 'Ok dear, I trust your judgement, but you are still very new to this, so how about we have a trial run, under my supervision. I will make you my 'concoction' as you put it, I call it reviver. Give me half an hour to make a batch and then we can try. Or maybe you could help me make it, it's a good idea for you to learn how to make it yourself in case you ever need it and I'm not here to make it for you.'

'Thanks Granny. That's a good idea, I'll come help.'

We went into the kitchen and Granny went to work. We crushed ingredients with a mortar and pestle, then added pinches of this and drops of that, then blessed some water and added it to the whole concoction. When it was done, it stunk to high heaven so I knew we had got it right. It seemed simple enough. I was pretty sure I could make it again myself. Granny's kitchen was well organised with everything labelled, so I wrote a list of all the ingredients down and the order in which to add them so I didn't forget. When it was all finished we had a jug full. It filled 13 smaller bottles. We put 12 of them in the fridge and then went back out to the clearing with Adam, Fiona and Lucas.

'Ok, so who's willing for me to rip your soul from your body?'

'When you put it like that, not me.' Adam said.

'Me either.' Fiona chimed in.

'It's alright, I'll volunteer, I already know what to expect and I trust you. Besides, floating was kind of fun. I found it relaxing.' Lucas said.

I smiled at him, grateful that he had so much faith in me.

'Ok, let's do this. Do you want to lie down so you don't fall again like you did the last time?' I asked.

'Yeah that's probably a good idea.'

'Wait don't lie on the ground, I'll get you a blanket to make you more comfortable and protect your clothes.' Granny said. She walked back into the house and returned a minute later with two large soft thick blankets with tartan print on the outside and fluffy on the inside and a pillow. She laid one out on the ground and put the pillow on top. Lucas lay on top of it and she put the other blanket over him. He raised his eyebrows.

'You might get cold lying there, can't have you getting hypothermia.' she said.

'Thanks.' he pulled the blanket up to his chin.

'Ok are you ready?' I asked.

'Wait Ashton. I think you should drink the reviver first. It will give you more energy.' Granny said.

'Ok, I guess so.' I said, pulling the bottle from my hoodie pocket and unscrewing the lid and lifting it to my lips. I screwed my face up at the foul smell and then downed it. I wondered if I would ever get used to the disgusting taste. I put the lid back on the bottle and put it back in my pocket. I instantly felt energy flowing through me, I was more alert and focused. So this is what it feels like when you haven't complete drained all your energy. I felt strong.

'Ready?' I asked, needing to do this before I lost my nerve.

'Ready.' Lucas confirmed.
I knelt beside him and closed my eyes. I found the strand of my spirit magic and pulled on it slowly, careful not to make any mistakes this time. I pushed my spirit magic into Lucas's chest feeling for his soul. He gasped at the touch of my magic, but he nodded to let me know he was ok. Fiona, Adam and Granny

watched on riveted. This time I recognised Lucas's soul as soon as my magic touched it. I slowly carefully wrapped the strand of my magic around it, then like ripping a band aid off tugged on it. The effect was instant. Lucas's face fell, his eyes closed his lashes touching his cheeks. He looked like he was in a peaceful sleep. 'That was a little less shocking than last time.' his voice came from beside me.

I turned to look at him. He stood beside me in spirit form, shimmering around the edges. 'Yes it's less shocking for me too considering I meant to do it this time.'

'Did it work?' Fiona whispered.

'Yes he's standing here beside me. He's ok. Right I'm going to try and put it back in now. Lucas I need you to lie down inside your body again.' He did as I asked. I could still see the shimmer of his spirit form.

I closed my eyes again and tugged on the black strand of magic that was becoming more familiar to me. I knew what I had to do this time, my panic last night overtook my common sense. I didn't need to start his heart again, I just needed to reattach his soul to his body with my magic, the same way I had removed it. Once I had my magic in my grasp, I pushed it out and I felt again for his soul, finding it almost instantly, he gasped in his spirit form. I wrapped my magic around both his soul and the part of his chest I had first found it and tied it off in knot. Then let go and opened my eyes, the shimmer of his spirit form was gone, he gasped and opened his eyes and smiled. 'I knew you could do it.'

'Thank God.' I breathed.

Every one laughed. I couldn't stop laughing. Relief making me delirious. I don't know how I knew what to do. I just knew it would work and it did.

'I can't believe you did that.' Granny said in awe. 'I've heard of necromancers having that kind of power, but they are few and far between.'

'You could have told me that before I tried Granny.' I said.

'You seemed so confident, I didn't want to burst your bubble.'

We all erupted into laughter again. Wiping away tears from his eyes, Lucas asked, 'How do you feel? Has it drained you?'

'I actually feel fine, I'm not sure if it was the reviver or I'm just getting more used to using my magic or if it's a combination of both, but I feel good.'

'I've never seen anything like it, you should be flat on your back in a coma after using that sort of power, especially being so new to this. You are acclimatising to your magic at a much faster rate than I've seen before. Do you think you can do it again?' Granny asked.
'I think so. Who wants to try next?' I asked.

'If Lucas can do it, I can do it better.' Adam said making us all laugh again.

Lucas got up from his position on the ground, he didn't seem to have any ill side effects which was encouraging. He passed the blanket that he had kept over him to Adam and Adam took his place lying on the blanket on the ground with the blanket on top of him.

'Ashton, if you kill me I will haunt you forever.' he smiled at me. Fiona and I both giggled and Granny rolled her eyes.

'Ok are you ready?' I asked.

'Go for it.' he replied.

I repeated the same thing again with Adam. It went just as smoothly as when I did it with Lucas. Well apart from Adam refusing to get back into his body so I could reattach his soul. He wanted to have fun in his spirit form first. He ran through Lucas and Fiona multiple times, giving them both the shivers. When he eventually agreed to get back inside his body the process was as quick and straight forward as it was with Lucas. What was more surprising was that it didn't significantly drain me.

'That was awesome.' Adam said as soon as he opened his eyes.

'Of course you would find fun in being dead.' I said dryly.

He rose from where he was lying on the ground to make space for Fiona.

'Are you going to try dear?' Granny asked Fiona.

Fiona took a deep breath. 'Yes ok I'll do it.' She took up Adam's position on the ground. She looked extremely anxious.

'Are you sure you're ok? You don't have to do this, we can just use Adam and Lucas.' I asked.

'Yes I'm fine, I want to help.' she said and I smiled at her.

'Ok, if you're sure.'

I closed my eyes and repeated the process again. I pulled Fiona's spirit from her body and she stood in spirit form beside it looking on in shock. 'This is such a strange sensation. I can still feel my body like I'm still tethered to it in some way, but also not at the same time. I feel like I'm floating.'

'You are floating.' I laughed looking at her ghostly feet hovering above the ground.

'Yeah I guess I am' she said as she glided about back and forward and around in circles. She went right up to Granny and waved her hand in her face and I laughed. 'This is so cool.' she said.
'Ok, well I'm glad you're enjoying yourself, but let's get your spirit reattached to your body, before I'm too tired to do it.' I said.

Fiona looked disappointed but lay down inside her own body and waited for me to reattach her spirit to her body. It took mere seconds and it was over. It was a bit anti-climatic, for me anyway as I was the one pulling the souls out and putting them back in. When her spirit was reattached she opened her eyes and slowly sat up. 'That was a lot more fun than I thought it would be.'

'I'm glad you have all enjoyed yourselves.' I said.

'I want a turn.' Granny said surprising us all

'Really? I'm not sure that's a good idea.' I worried.

'Oh, is that right? And why not? Because I'm old?' Granny asked sternly.

'Oh er, no, that's not what I meant at all, I erm, it was just in case something goes wrong.' I stumbled over my words.

Granny laughed. 'Just get on with it, I'll be fine.' She lay down on the blanket and I repeated the same process again, carefully pulling her soul from her body. Granny smiled with wonder, she zoomed from one side of the clearing to the other. Then she went right up in to Adam's face and shouted at the top of her voice 'Boo!'. Adam didn't so much as flinch, though I think he could sense her near by. I burst out laughing. Only Granny.

After another few minutes, she got back into her body and I reattached her soul. She was up on her feet within in seconds. 'I can't wait for an excuse to do that again.' she said. 'How do you feel now Ashton?' she added.

'Strangely I feel completely fine. Taking the reviver before I started must have helped. It might all hit me at once later.'

'Take it easy for now. I think we should let Mia know what we've been up to. I don't know her friends and I'm still wary of whether we can trust anyone, so I want to keep this on a need to know basis. Let's tell only family and Mia for now.' Granny said.

'That makes sense.'

Back inside Granny told everyone to make themselves comfortable. Adam, Lucas, Fiona, Mia, Courtney, Emily, Leanne and Michael went into the games room. Whilst my Mum, Leona, Aunt Emma, Uncle Mark and Uncle Malcolm went to the sitting room. Granny and I stayed in the kitchen to make tea for everyone. When it was ready I went into the games room and asked Mia to come and help me carry it into the games room.

'So what's going on?' Mia asked.

'How did you know?' I replied.

'You haven't exactly been covert. You cooked up a batch of something disgusting and you all disappeared for an hour, I knew you were up to something. Are you planning on poisoning the necromancers?' she laughed.

'No, it's a little bit crazier than that. It turns out with my necromancer abilities I can pull a person's soul out and turn them into a spirit for a little while, then put it back in.'

Mia's eyes widdened. 'Why would you want to do that?'

'It would be insane to go in blind to bring Sophia back. So the plan was for Adam, Lucas, Fiona and I to check out Dunluce Castle and The Marine Hotel to see if Sophia is being held. But as soon as they see us it's game over. So the idea is to get close enough without being noticed and for me to pull their souls from their bodies and they can check the place out unnoticed as spirits. Then go to the other and do the same.' I looked at Mia expectantly.

'You're nuts. Even if you could do that, it wouldn't work. If you can see spirits then other necromancers will too and then our cover is blown.'

'Well that's the thing. Granny said most necromancer's can't see spirits, only the very powerful ones can. But even if there are powerful necromancers there that can see spirits, they won't be expecting us to use spirits to spy on them. It's kind of perfect.'

'I guess so. Are you sure you want to do this? I mean are you sure you *can* do this? It seems really risky.'

'I've just removed Adam, Lucas, Fiona and Granny's spirits from their bodies and then reattached them. They're all fine. I wouldn't suggest it if I thought I couldn't do it.'

'You pulled your Granny's spirit from her body?' Mia asked shocked.

'She asked me to. She didn't want to be left out.' I laughed.

'How are you still standing? That seems like a lot of powerful magic to use at once?'

'Well that's what we were making before hand. Reviver. I passed out when I did it last night and the reviver brought me around. We have 12 bottles of it prepared. I think we should be good.'

'I'm relying on a headcase to help me get my sister back.' Mia rolled her eyes and laughed.

'You're welcome.' I said sarcastically.

'Thanks. So when are you guys going to do this?'

'I think everyone should stay here tonight. When everyone goes to bed, we can sneak out. Then come tomorrow if we have Sophia's location, we're prepared for going in.'

'Why are we sneaking out?' Mia asked.

'We?'

'Yes, I'm going with you, you need me. If Fiona, Lucas and Adam are spirits what if someone attacks you and you aren't able to reattach their spirits to their bodies, or if you pass out. You need backup.'

'I didn't think of that. Ok, you're in. As for why we're sneaking out, sorry but we don't know your friends, and after what happened with Sophia, we are trying to be more careful with who we trust.'

'Ok fair enough, I'll keep it quiet.'

'We better get back or everyone will be looking for us. Help me carry this would you?'

The rest of the evening was spent waiting, even though I knew even if Granny heard anything back she wasn't going to say anything until we had completed our scouting mission. That's why we had to go tonight. So whilst everyone else was waiting for word of Sophia's location, Mia, Fiona, Adam, Lucas and I were waiting until everyone went to bed so we could sneak out.

I feigned tiredness at around 10pm and said I was going to get an early night. I loaded up with snacks and drinks and bottles of reviver and put them in the dumbwaiter and sent them upstairs. Michael and Leanne and Adam went to bed at the same time as me. Once the last of Mia's friends went to bed, everyone else was to meet in my bedroom, but they had to wait until they were all gone first.

I made my way upstairs and lifted the drinks and snacks and reviver from the dumbwaiter and went into my room. I got a backpack from my wardrobe and started loading it up. I put 3 bottles of reviver in the front pocket wrapped in a t-shirt to prevent them from breaking and I put another 2 in each of my hoodie pockets. I would drink one before I left.

Adam came into my room first, forgetting to knock as usual. He knew Mia was coming from our brief whispered conversations downstairs. 'So what's the deal? Why is Mia tagging along.' he asked flopping down on my bed.

I rolled my eyes. 'Mia isn't tagging along. She's coming to help. Whilst you are all going to sneak around and spy she's going to stay with me to help protect me and your bodies in case we're caught. She has more motivation than anyone for this to work because she wants to get her sister back. We haven't filled in Emily, Courtney, Leanne and Michael as the less people who know the better, I'm still not sure who we can trust.'

'Ok that makes sense.' he said. 'I guess we just have to wait for them. How would you like to pass the time?' he grinned at me.

I rolled my eyes again, he seemed to have that affect on me. 'Here, I brought you snacks, lets watch something on TV whilst we wait.' I threw the rest of the snacks that didn't fit in my back pack to Adam then gave him the TV remote and sat on the bed beside him with the pillows propped up behind me. He opened a sharing packet of crisps and began crunching away whilst flicking through the TV channels. 'Hey don't get any crumbs on my bed.'

He threw a crisp at me in response. 'Adam I'm going to kill you, stop it. I have to sleep in this bed tonight.'

The door knocked, putting an end to our arguing. 'Come in.' I called.

Fiona, Lucas and Mia filed in. I got that familiar jolt when I laid my eyes on Lucas.

'This looks cosy.' Mia said making my face go red, which made me look guilty even though it was completely innocent. Annoyance flashed across Lucas's face. Great, I can't win.

'So what's the plan?' Fiona asked.

'Has everyone else gone to bed?' I asked.

'Yeah I think so.' she replied.

'We're good to go if you guys are?' I said.

'I was thinking we should maybe grab some weapons from the library.' Lucas said.

'Are you planning on fighting anyone whilst you're unconscious?' I laughed.

'No but you and Mia might need to. It's good to be prepared.'

'Ok I suppose you're right.' I remembered how the throwing stars had saved us last time.

We quietly creeped out of my room and into the library which thankfully was empty. We loaded up with weapons, I took another pair throwing stars and I had already got the Sgian Dubh from my room and attached it in my ankle holster. Mia took a short sword and Adam took a pair of throwing stars that matched mine. Fiona and Lucas took matching daggers. I could only hope that the police didn't pull us over. That would completely derail our plans.

CHAPTER 16

When we were loaded up with weapons we crept quietly out to my car and made the journey to Dunluce Castle Ruins. Although the necromancers had made it more habitable, with tarpaulin protecting them from the elements, the castle was still in ruins, a lot of it had fell off the cliff into the sea hundreds of years ago, so it wasn't an ideal place for their base or to keep prisoners. It was just a front I now realised.

When we arrived we pulled up in the same lay by as before, far enough away that we wouldn't be seen but close enough that we didn't have too far too travel.

Mia sat in the passenger seat beside me. Once I cut the engine, I took my seatbelt off and turned to look at Adam, Fiona and Lucas in the back. 'Ok, are you guys ready?' I asked.

When everyone agreed they were ready I reminded them what they needed to do. 'Ok so we need to know how many necromancers are here, if Sophia is here, where they are keeping her and any other information that might come in useful.'

I opened my bag and unrolled the t-shirt that held three bottles of reviver. I took one bottle out and rolled the other two back up and placed them back in the front pocket of my bag. I still had the two bottles in my hoodie pockets as I wanted to keep them ready to hand in case anything should go wrong and I needed them quickly. I opened the bottle and drank it quickly hoping that it would diminish the god awful taste. No such luck. I instantly felt invigorated though and ready for anything.

I started with Adam this time, then Lucas and then finally Fiona. Once they were all in spirit form inside the car seemed very crowded. It was strange to watch them all go through the solid walls of the car out into the open air. They moved very quickly as spirits and were out of sight in seconds.

Mia who had turned in her seat to watch, stared transfixed at the three motionless bodies in the back of the Range Rover. 'Are you sure they're going to be ok?' she asked. 'They look dead.'

'I hope so.' I said without thinking.

'What do you mean you hope so? I thought you knew what you were doing?' she panicked.

'I didn't mean that. They will be fine. I've done this multiple times now, I know exactly how to reattach their spirits to their bodies. Let's just hope they bring us back some useful information.'

Mia relaxed and we waited in the eery silence, watching and waiting for any sign of being spotted by the necromancers or for Adam, Lucas and Fiona returning. We had been waiting for what felt like forever but was only actually around 30 minutes when Adam returned first. 'Ashton, we've got to get down there, they have a prisoner.'

'Is it Sophia?' I asked, instantly becoming alert when Adam appeared in spirit form.

'What's going on?' Mia asked, unable to see or hear Adam.

'Give me a minute.' I said.

'No it was a man, his head is covered so I didn't see his face.' Adam said.

'It's not Sophia, there's a male prisoner, Adam is going back to help him.' I said to Mia.

'Put me back in my body so I can go help him.' Adam said.

'Ok. Get back inside your body quickly.' Adam got back inside his body and I tied his spirit to it.

Adam lifted his head, opened his eyes and took his first gasping breath. 'Come on, we've got to go. He is unattended at the moment but they could come back.'

'Adam I can't leave Fiona and Lucas's bodies here. What if something happens to them?'

'Ok, you're right, I can go alone. There's about 18 necromancers scattered here, low level, I don't think much is happening here, other than the prisoner. Hopefully Fiona and Lucas will be back soon. I'm going to go now.'

'Be careful Adam.' I said.

'Aww are you worried about me?' he said.
'A momentary lapse. I'm over it, you can go now.'

He laughed and got out of the car and ran down the road out of sight.

'I wonder what's keeping Fiona and Lucas?' I said getting anxious.

'I've been thinking the same thing.' Mia replied. 'Isn't there like a ghost call or something you can do to call them back?'

I laughed, Mia glared at me. I held my hands up, 'Relax, I thought you were joking. Though it would come in handy. But no, not as far as I'm aware. I've no way of calling spirits. Hey, I think I see them.' Before I had even finished speaking I could see two spirits moving towards us that I hoped were Lucas and Fiona.

'Is it them?.' Mia asked excitedly.

When they reached the car they glided through the doors, I don't think I'd ever get used to seeing that.

'Ashton, you're never going to believe what we've found. There are massive tunnels underneath the castle that go for miles. It's like someone has built hundreds of apartments inside caves under the castle. There's only one entrance from the castle itself, its under the ruins of the old spires. We seen at least 50 necromancers down there.' Fiona said clearly disturbed by what she had seen.

'Let's get you both back inside your bodies then we can talk.'

After putting both their spirits back inside their bodies Lucas realised that Adam's body was no longer there. 'Where did Adam go?' he asked.

'He said they have a prisoner, he's going to help them. He wouldn't wait until you guys came back. I didn't want to leave your bodies unattended. We have to go and help him but I don't know where he is. Did you see the prisoner?'

'No we didn't see anyone. Adam went off doing his own thing. We stuck together and after a few minutes of looking around we found the tunnels. We never would have found them inside our bodies. Unfortunately there was no sign of Sophia, I don't know if that's a good thing or a bad thing.'

'Adam didn't find her either.' I said. 'We need to go help him before he's discovered.'

'Come on, we will all go, as long as you're feeling alright that is?' Lucas asked.

'Yes, I'm totally fine, the reviver is doing its job. Let's go.'

We all got out of the car and quietly jogged to the entrance of the castle and stopped to look around to make sure no one was watching. Once we were sure we hadn't been seen we walked down the pathway to the bridge. Mia and I split from Lucas and Fiona, they went to the left and we went to right, splitting up to cover more ground. There was a steep downwards slope in front of us or a steep incline to the side, we chose the slope, trying to walk down it carefully to avoid slipping. I got to the bottom first and held my hand out for Mia to help steady her over the uneven ground. I didn't know which way to go so I decided to work from the outside inwards. The ruins on the outside were right on the edge of the cliff. We walked around the perimeter, not needing to look inside every room because the windowless frames allowed us to poke our heads through and take a look. I started to think these rooms weren't isolated or secure enough to keep a prisoner and was about to tell Mia that we were probably looking in the wrong place, when Adam appeared to our right, he was practically dragging the prisoner, the prisoner's arm over his shoulder and Adams arm around his back and under his arm pit, the prisoner's feet dragging along the ground, his head hanging on his chest. When Adam seen us he looked relieved, but was careful not to make any noise. We ran over and helped support the prisoner's weight from the other side. He looked in bad shape. We just needed to get out of here before being spotted, but I had no idea how we were getting him up this hill. I held my hand up to get Adam and Mia to stop for second and grabbed my phone from my pocket and sent a text message to both Lucas and Fiona to say we had found Adam and the prisoner and to meet us at the car. When I put my phone back in the pocket of my hoodie it hit off something. It was the small bottle of reviver, then I had an idea. I took the bottle out and handed it to Lucas, he looked at me questioningly. 'Drink it for energy then use your air magic to lift him up the hill, I'll help.' I whispered. I put my hand in my other pocket and lifted the other bottle and drank it as quickly as I could, instantly feeling the effects. Adam opened his and downed it as well and then gave me the thumbs up. We both pulled on our air magic and pushed it up beneath all of our feet, our combined magic being more than enough to easily float us all up to the top of the hill, but we didn't stop there, needing to get out quickly and without being seen, we floated the rest of the way up over the bridge and up the pathway until we got to the road. Once there we both gently eased off our air magic until we were all eased back onto our feet, well apart from the prisoner. Now that we were on even ground, Adam put the prisoner up over his shoulder and ran the rest of the way to the car with Mia and I running behind him making sure he didn't fall. Lucas and Fiona were already at the car when we got there. I ran ahead and opened the back door so that Adam could lay the prisoner down on the back seat. He seemed completely unconscious. When Adam lay him down I instantly recognised the prisoner through his swollen beaten face and gasped. 'It's the book shop owner.'

'I know.' was all Adam said.

'What would the necromancers want with the owner of a bookshop?' Fiona asked.

'I don't know, but we have to get him back to Granny's house. He doesn't look good. There's two extra seats in the boot. Can we sit him upright and two of you sit in there to give him space.'

'Lucas and I can get in the back.' Fiona said.

Adam went to the passenger side back door and opened then grabbed the prisoner under the arms and pulled him back to sit up right on the end seat, all the while he didn't stir. This allowed Fiona to press the button on the other side to move the seats forward and bring out the extra seats in the boot. This car was like a transformer. Fiona and Lucas got in the back seats and Adam walked around and got in behind the drivers seat. Mia and I got in the front again and then we were off. It was lucky that we weren't caught because if the necromancers were aware of our involvement they might have guessed what we were up to. Now they wouldn't' know who had freed the prisoner or if he had freed himself.

When we got back to Granny's house I parked as close to the front door as possible. Mia ran in ahead to let Granny know we needed help. Adam got out and let Fiona and Lucas out of the back seat and him and Lucas went around and lifted the prisoner into the house. I got them to bring him in and lay him down on the pool table, as I thought Granny would prefer that to her nice sofa.

Granny rushed in after Mia with Mum, Leona and Auntie Emma.

'What's happened?' Granny said.

'The necromancers were keeping him prisoner, he is the owner of the book store in Bushmills. Adam found him in spirit form and then went back to free him. He looks badly beaten, he's been unconscious the whole time.'

'Let me get a look, Fiona dear pass me a cushion from the sofa please so I can prop his head up.' Everyone crowded around. My Mum gasped her face a mask of complete and utter horror and shock.

'Mum, what's wrong?' I asked worriedly. She just continued to stare, seeming not to hear me. Granny glanced at her curiously.

'Mum for goodness sake tell us what's wrong, you're scaring me.' I said panicking now.

She looked at me and whispered. 'That's Gavin, he's your Father.'

CHAPTER 17

Reeling from the bombshell my Mum had just dropped on me, I walked out of the games room in a daze and out through the back of the house to the clearing and I knelt on my knees on the ground like I had done the night of my ceremony. I don't know what possessed me to do it but I begged my ancestors, please don't let my Dad be evil, please let my Dad be ok, please help me. Over and over and over again in my head whilst tears trickled down my face.

'Ashton, we all have the capacity for good and for evil, it is our choices that matter. You already have the power to heal him, but you must go now, you need him to save.' A voice drifted on the air, I looked around but I couldn't see anyone.

'Hello? How can I save him?' I said out loud to the air surrounding me.

'You must go.' the voice said again urgently.

So I went. I got up and ran as fast as I could back into the house through the kitchen and into the games room.

Granny's eyes met mine. With a sad look on her face she said,

'I'm sorry Ashton, I don't think there is anything more I can do, his injuries are too extensive.'

I looked back at her with pure determination and stubbornness, and said 'I can do it.'

I walked over to him, his skin was grey, with his eyes closed he looked dead already, his face so swollen and bruised on one side he was barely recognisable. I laid one hand on his head and the other on his chest and closed my eyes. I pulled on the black strand of spirit magic and pushed it out through my hands, I felt with my magic, amazed that I could feel the broken bones, the internal bleeding, the swelling and the blood loss, I could also feel how shallow his breathing was and knew that I needed to act fast, his heart was weak. I pushed my magic anywhere I could feel swelling and gently very gently so I didn't disrupt his soul, pulled it back out towards myself. This time I could feel the drain, I kept going though, not wanting to leave any swelling on his brain, I repaired his punctured lung pulling it into myself until nothing not even a scar was left, again with his cracked sternum and his broken fingers, his broken jaw again and again for every injury, not willing to leave anything behind that might cause him to die before I got to know him. Dizziness was taking over but I couldn't' stop.

'Ashton, that's enough.' Mum said placing her hand on my arm, I opened my eyes, colour had returned to his face, his breathing was more even and the bruising and swelling were all but gone.

'That's impossible.' I whispered.

'You healed him,' Mum said softly.

I breathed a sigh of relief and let go of my magic that I was holding on to so tightly. The release made me sag, my Mum putting her arm around me to help hold me upright and lead me to the sofa. When I sat down I looked around and every one was transfixed on either me or Gavin.

Adam stormed out of the room, wondering what was wrong I looked after him but the head movement made me woozy. The room was spinning, I needed to lie down. Adam rushed back into the room with something in his hand. I recognised it through my grogginess, it was a bottle of reviver, he unscrewed the top and handed it to me and I drank it, immediately regretting it because of the fowl taste but also immediately feeling more alert and energised. The room stopped spinning. 'Thank you.' I smiled at him.

'That was the most amazing thing I've ever seen. You're my hero.' he grinned at me.

'Mine too,' a raspy voice said and my head whipped around to see Gavin trying to sit himself up on the pool table. 'Thank you Ashton.'

I stood and walked over to him. His eyes filled with unshed tears. 'I'm so sorry I missed our meeting. This wasn't exactly how I had planned meeting you for the first time.' He turned to look at my Mum, she looked conflicted, about whether to slap him or go to him. 'Maureen, I'm sorry, I know I said I would stay away, but Ashton is in danger and I wanted to warn her, unfortunately it was discovered that I had planned to meet with her and I was detained before I got that chance.'

'What do you mean she's in danger?' Mum barked at him.

'Mum! Relax.' I said.

She nodded. She seemed to be having difficulty controlling her emotions.

Gavin swung his legs over the side of the pool table and stood, wincing a little. He limped over to where my Mum stood beside me. She looked up into his face and then she slapped him. The sound echoed through the quiet games room, everyone too stunned to speak. She fled out of the room.

'I deserved that.' Gavin smiled sadly. 'May I sit down?' he asked. I nodded and he sat down next to me.

'Right,' Granny interrupted loudly. 'Everyone clear out.'

Everyone left except for Adam and Granny, 'I will be right outside if you need me.' he said.

'I'll be right with him.' Granny added.

'Thank you, both of you.' Adam nodded as they left.

'So I'm sure by now you will have heard who and what I am.'

'Yes and I've just now realised why you were so weird that day I came into your shop, you already knew who I was. How?'

He laughed. 'Yes I guess you're right in that assessment. I was completely taken off guard by the daughter who I had dreamt about for most of my adult life, just walking into my shop to buy some books. I knew who you were because despite my better judgement I couldn't help but keep tabs on you over the years.'

'Ok. Before we go any further, I need to know. Are you evil?'

He burst out laughing. 'Would an evil person tell you if they're evil?'

I couldn't help but laugh too. 'No I suppose they wouldn't.'

'We all have the capacity for good and evil. It is our choices that matter.' he said.

'Where did you hear that? Someone said those exact words to me tonight.'

'Harry Potter, Order of the Phoenix.' he said solemnly.

'You're kidding right?'

'Nope.'

We both cracked up laughing. When I was finally able to speak again I said 'This isn't how I saw this going.'

'Me either. But it's great to see you laugh. There are some things that I really must tell you though Ashton.'

'Go for it.'

'For over two hundred years necromancers and druids have been enemies.' he began.

I held my hand up to stop him. 'I've heard this all before, necromancers died during the Typhus Epidemic and then the less powerful necromancer's tried to bring them back and drained the land causing the Irish Potato Famine, which in turn caused a war with the druids.'

'Yes you are well informed. But before that, necromancers and druids worked closely together, we were allies. Some of us want that again. We are not all just trying to grasp at power. Though I will admit there are many that are, most are good people just like druids.'

'Why should I believe you?' I asked.

'Well, I had hoped that by keeping your existence a secret from the necromancers your whole life that might go a way towards helping you and your Mum trust me. But there is also another very well kept secret amongst us, I am very powerful, as are my family, so I have no need to seek power. There are very few powerful necromancers left and the ones that are left mostly hide their power.'

'But why? That doesn't make sense.' I asked confused.

'Because if you are one of a minority that has the power that others so desperately seek, then you are likely to be used for that power. But there is a secret about where that power comes from, powerful necromancers come from mixing our bloodlines with druids. We have always been close, so close that many of us married. In older times when a female druid married a necromancer, they were no longer called druids they became necromancers through marriage, and it worked the same way with female necromancers who married a druid, they became druids through marriage. This was the norm. It has taken quite a bit of research for us to learn this information. Necromancers and Druid families who have had mixed 'race' relations we'll call it are the families who have remained powerful, the bigoted families that did not believe in mixed race relations have weakened. Your family remains powerful more than two hundred years later because you are of mixed blood, and you are now the most powerful druid and necromancer in recent times because you have directly mixed blood.'

'How does no one else know this?'

'I have dedicated a lot of my life to research. I am a bit of a book worm as you probably already noticed, history interests me, more so after meeting your mother and conceiving you, I wanted to understand why Druids and Necromancers had to be enemies. I want you to know that I loved your mother. I deceived her and that was wrong, but it was only because I was afraid she wouldn't accept me for what I was. In the end she didn't accept me because I hid the truth from her. It's the biggest regret of my life.'

I tried to push down the lump forming in my throat, wishing things could have been different and that I could have grown up with a Father.

He continued. 'There's more. Now that the necromancers know that you have their blood and their power, they want to use you. They were watching the house when I delivered my note to ask you to meet with me, they wanted to know why I was here, so they kidnapped and tortured me. I didn't give them any information, but I don't think it will take them long to figure it out that I'm your Father. Spirit's of our ancestors have told them of a saviour coming, with both Druidic and Necromancer blood that will save their bloodline.'

'Wait, do you know about the book?'

'What book?' he asked confused.

'There has been a book in my Granny's library for centuries and it could only be opened by an 'heir' using blood magic. My blood is the only blood that opens the book, but the book was stolen from the house. The book said something about the heir being the only one to wield the fifth power to save the bloodline.'

'Interesting, it sounds the same as what the ancestors are telling the necromancers. But it only confirms the reason I was worried and what I was trying to warn you about. I'm afraid they're going to come to the conclusion that you are the one who is going to save their bloodline.'

'But then why did they steal the book if they knew that only I could open it?' I asked.

'I would guess they are trying other options to open the book and if all else fails, they will come back for you.'

'We thought as much. But it still leaves me wondering how they knew about the book in the first place.'

'That I can't answer. It is possible that you have a leak here amongst the Druids. Can you think of who it might be?'

'There were only four people that knew about the book, one of them was me, the others were Granny, Mum and Lucas and I don't think any of them betrayed me.'

'You must be careful Ashton. It may be someone that you would not suspect.'

'Yeah I guess so.'

'I'm grateful to have had this chance to speak with you. Would you mind if we talked again soon?'

'No I don't mind.' I said meaning it.

'I don't currently have a phone, the necromancers have taken it, but if you could write your phone number down for me, then I will get in touch as soon as I have a new one.'

'Sure I'll go and write it down for you. Give me a minute.'

'Ashton, before you go, I was hoping to speak to your Mother.' he looked at me hopefully.

I smiled, 'I will ask her, but I can't promise anything.'

'Thank you, and thank you for saving my life, I wouldn't be here without you.'

'You're welcome.'

I left the room to find, Granny, Adam, Lucas and Fiona right outside the door. They had obviously been listening to every word, so now the secret was out about the book. Granny went to the console table in the hall and opened the drawer and handed me a pen and a page from a notepad. I smiled gratefully at her and wrote my number down on the piece of paper. I went back and gave it to Gavin then returned and asked 'Where's Mum?'

'She's in the sitting room with your Aunt Emma and Leona.' Granny answered.

'Thanks Granny.' I said walking into the sitting room.
My Mum looked up when I entered. Aunt Emma and Leona got up from their seats, and walked to the door, smiling at me as they passed.

'Are you ok sweetheart?' Mum asked.

'Yes I'm good actually. He wants to talk to you.'

Mum looked at me blankly for a second. 'I don't know if I should. He can't be trusted, I've already been sucked into his lies in the past.'

'For what it's worth, I think we can trust him. I think you should talk to him Mum.' She nodded and stood and squeezed my arm as she left the room.

I sat for a moment alone taking it all in. I met my Dad, I saved my Dad's life, my Dad wasn't evil.

'Hey, are you ok?' It was Lucas.

I smiled at him. 'I'm ok, just trying to process everything that just happened.'

'It has been an eventful day. There seems to be a lot of those with you around.' he laughed.

'I guess that's true. My life used to be so normal.'

'Normal is boring. I think it would do you good to get some rest, all of us actually.'

'But we still don't know where Sophia is.'

'It will have to wait until tomorrow. You need sleep before you use any more of your magic. We can go to the Marine Hotel tomorrow night.'

'I suppose so.'

'Come on.' He pulled me up by the hand and wrapped his arms around me giving me the tingles.

'Smooth.' I said.

He laughed. 'Let's get you to bed.'

I raised my eyebrows at him and he bent his head to kiss me. I leant into his kiss and wrapped my arms around him not wanting to let go, pushing down the electric shock sensations that kissing him caused, not wanting to burn him again.

'Hey, oh sorry to interrupt.' it was Fiona.

I looked up just in time to see Adam walk out of the room. I could feel my face go crimson. At not only being caught in the act, but at obviously upsetting Adam too. I took a step back from Lucas, squeezing his hand to let him know it wasn't him. He smiled at me turned to face Fiona.

'Hey Fiona, great timing.'

'Sorry how was I supposed to know you'd be sucking each other's faces. We just came to see if Ashton was ok, but it looks like I'm on my own now.'

'Thanks Fiona, I'm fine. I was just about to head to bed. I guess we will have to wait until tomorrow to go to the Marine Hotel.'

'I think that's the best idea. I'm wiped so I can only imagine how you feel.'

I laughed, 'Not as bad as expected, the reviver is doing its job. Anyway I'm off to bed. Good night.'

'Good night.' Fiona and Lucas said at the same time and then they both laughed at the same time.

'Creepy.' I replied shaking my head as I left the room.

I got a much needed shower when I got back to my room and got dressed in shorts and t-shirt pajamas. I knew I was tired, but I also knew I wasn't going to sleep any time soon. I met my Dad tonight. I didn't know what to make of that, but I did know one thing, I believed everything he said, he did love my Mum.

I lay down on my bed and turned the TV on and began aimlessly flicking through the channels.

There was a knock on my door. 'Come in.'

My Mum poked her head around the door. 'Hey, are you alright?'

'I'm fine, you don't need to keep asking me that. And since when have you knocked?'

Mum laughed, 'Sorry you're right. It's been a big day.'

'Are you ok?' I asked.

'Yes, I'm alright. I just don't really know what to think. I want to believe what Gavin is saying but he's lied to me before.'

'I believe him. Maybe it's because I'm new to all this so I have an outsider's perspective, but I don't believe all necromancers are bad, just like I don't believe all druids are good. We're all just people, why are we still enemies two hundred years later because of the sins of our ancestors. Do you have a good reason to dislike necromancers other than that's what was taught to you since you were a child?'

My Mum looked at me in surprise. 'You're right, it's nothing more than bigotry that's been passed down through the generations and now I'm trying to pass it on to you. I've never really thought of it like that, but you worded it perfectly.'

'It's just how I see it. As for Gavin, I feel like he is genuine and that he cares about us. I want to get to know him, but I also don't want to upset you.'

'As long as his intentions aren't in question then I won't get in your way. But please just be careful.'

'I will, thanks Mum.'

'Ok well I'm going to let you get some sleep, I'm sure you need it after tonight. I've never seen anything like what you done tonight, by all rights, Gavin should be dead.'

'Is it weird for you that I have necromancer abilities?' I asked, curious.

'No, because you're using them to do good which is what being a druid is about.' she smiled at me and turned and left the room.

I went back to my channel flicking unable to pay attention, a million thoughts running through my head. I got up without thinking about where I was going and before I knew it I was knocking on the door to the room Lucas was staying in.

The door swung open on Lucas pulling a t-shirt over his head. He smiled when his eyes met mine, 'Hey Ashton, you ok? Do you want to come in?' he said standing back and holding his arm out gesturing me into the room.

'Thanks.' I said walking into the room. It was the room decorated in silver that I had first looked at when I got here. It had a similar layout to my room it was just a little smaller with a smaller wardrobe.

Lucas walked over and sat on the bed. I sat on the armchair beside the bed and looked at him awkwardly.

'So, what's up?' Lucas asked breaking the silence.

'Nothing, I just couldn't sleep and I didn't want to be alone.' I said.

'That's understandable. Do you want to watch a film?'

'That depends. What film?'

'What about my favourite, Home Alone?'

I laughed,'I wasn't expecting you to say that. I love that film.'

'Come here.' he said.

I stood up and walked over to where he sat on the bed. He stood up and lifted me like I weighed nothing and laid me down on the bed, then he propped my pillows up behind me.

'Do you want a blanket?' he asked.

'Yeah thanks.'

He walked into the wardrobe and got a light blanket and came and tucked it in around me, making sure my feet were covered and tucking it up right under my chin like I was a little kid. It was nice. Then he took his shoes off and lay down beside me making sure to stay on his own side of the bed. A little too gentlemanly for my liking, but it was still sweet. He put the film on and we watched it while he pointed out all his favourite bits. Lucas was a lot more open and talkative one on one. When the film was over we watched the second one. At some point we must have dozed off. I woke up to daylight streaming through the window in Lucas's room and realised that we were holding hands. Lucas was still peacefully asleep. Not wanting to disturb him I tried to unlink our fingers. He opened his eyes and smiled. 'Good morning.'

'Morning, I was trying not to wake you.' I said.

'It's ok I like waking up with you.' he said.

Awkward.

'Yeah it's ok.' I said, instantly regretting it.

He burst out laughing and I couldn't help laughing too, lightening the mood.

'I better go get dressed. Do you want to get some breakfast?' I asked.

'Yeah, I'll see you in a few.'

As I left Lucas's room and closed the door I bumped right into Adam in the hallway.

'Oh sorry Adam.'

He looked me up and down and took in my pajamas and shook his head in disgust and stormed off without a word.

Realising how it must have looked I called after him, 'Adam wait.' But he had already rounded the corner down the spiral staircase.

I sighed, annoyed how something so innocent had been taken out of context. Great just what I needed, now Adam was pissed off at me.

I went to my room to get ready, I brushed my teeth and got dressed and grabbed my phone off the charger and checked the time. It was 10.30 am. I was glad I hadn't slept too late for once. It would give me more time to plan for the day. I also wanted to find Adam and do damage control.

I went downstairs to find Granny in the kitchen, big surprise there, Fiona was here too. 'Good morning.'

Granny and Fiona both looked up at me surprised. 'Morning Ashton, you look great. I was half expecting you to sleep half the day and need some reviver to get you up and about.' Granny said.

'I didn't even think of that.' I said.

'You are becoming accustomed to using your abilities at an alarming rate.'

'Well the reviver last night probably had something to do with that.' I said. 'Has anyone seen Adam?' I added.

'He went out back a little while ago, he didn't seem too happy. He's probably still annoyed about seeing you and Lucas kissing last night.' Fiona said.

'You and Lucas?' Granny said with raised eyebrows. 'That explains Adam's mood, he didn't even want any breakfast. Let him down gently Ashton.'

'I know, *I know*.' I said rubbing my face with my hands. 'I don't want to upset anyone. I'm going to go and find him.' I said exiting to the yard where the outbuildings where. I walked out past them to the clearing. When I didn't see Adam I took the lane to the old Castle, when the lane forked I went to the left, it opened into the clearing that held the castle. I loved this place. I stopped for a second to take it all in when I noticed movement to my left at the tree line. There Adam sat on a large rock, staring into space. When I looked at him, it was like he had sensed my presence. He turned to look at me as I slowly approached. When I reached him I nudged his shoulder with mine. 'Can I sit here?'

'It's not my rock, you can sit where you like.' he said grumpily.

I sat down beside him and rested my head on his shoulder. I could feel him relax. 'I'm sorry Adam. I didn't mean for any of this to happen, or to upset you.'

'I know I don't have any right to be angry.'
'I understand. But you're the best friend I have and I don't think I could survive if you hated me.'

'Great, so I've been friend zoned.' he chuckled.

'It's not like that. Lucas just kissed me and it was nice.'

'So you slept with him.' he stated matter of a fact.

'No! I didn't sleep with him. Well I mean I slept with him, as in I fell asleep, but we were fully clothed, we didn't have sex, we just watched films until we fell asleep.'

'Oh. I just assumed.' he said.

'Well you were wrong.'

'I'm sorry. I'm also sorry I haven't even asked you if you're ok after meeting your Dad and pretty much bringing him back from the brink of death. That was insane. I've been selfish and only thinking about how I feel.'

'It's ok, I'm fine. That's why I was with Lucas last night, I just couldn't sleep and wanted some company.'

'You could have came to me for company.' he said in annoyance.

'Could I have? You stormed out of the living room when you seen

Lucas and I together. I'd had my limit on drama for the day.'

'Ok that's fair enough, I get your point. I'll drop it. Though I did want to ask you about something else. I listened at the door last night when you were talking to your Dad and heard you talking about the book. Why didn't you tell me?'

'Granny said to not tell anyone else, as we didn't know who we could trust after Sophia betraying us.'

'And you didn't think you could trust me? But you still told Lucas.'

'No it wasn't that at all. I was with Lucas when I opened the book for the first time, that's how he knew, so afterwards I told Mum and Granny together and they said not to tell anyone else.'

'So if only you, Lucas, your Mum and Granny knew about the book, how did the necromancers find out?'

'I don't know, I wondered if it was Lucas. But we asked him and he said it wasn't him and I believed him. He said he knew if anything happened to the book that suspicion would fall on him. It just doesn't add up for it to be him.'

'Or it's the perfect excuse.' He said.
'Do you think Lucas would do something like that?' I asked.

'I don't know. I don't know Lucas all that well anymore. We were friends before he went travelling, but since he came back he's been different, quieter I guess. If you had asked me back then the answer would have been a definite no. Though to be honest, I can't think of any reason why he would work with the necromancers. Unless I'm missing something.'

'I can't think of any reason he would either, but then again

Sophia did. We need to make a plan to go to the Marine Hotel to see if she's there.'

'Did your Granny hear back from her contact? She might know where Sophia is already.'

'Even if she does, we still need to check the place out. But still we should go and ask her.'

'Ok, let's go. But before we do' he didn't finish his sentence. Instead he turned and cupped my face in his hands and he kissed me. Everything else fell away, I kissed him back, forgetting all the reasons why I shouldn't. His lips were soft but firm against mine, I melted against him, feeling my fire magic sizzle under the surface of my skin. He broke it off too soon, leaving me wanting more. I smiled at him, our foreheads still touching.

'That was unexpected.' I said still breathless.

'I just wanted to even the playing field, so you're fully informed before you make any rash decisions.'

I laughed, then panic set in. 'Oh god what am I doing? Adam this is a mess. I shouldn't have kissed you.'

His face dropped.

'No I don't mean it like that. But I kissed Lucas and pissed you off, and now that we have kissed that's probably going to piss off Lucas. I don't like this. I already felt guilty before, now I feel even worse about what I'm doing to both of you.'

'No one said you have to tell Lucas, I can be your dirty secret.' he said wiggling his eyebrows and making me laugh again.

'Can you just be serious for once? We can't do this. You and Lucas are friends, you and I are friends, and Lucas and I are, well I don't know what we are, I guess we were never really friends, but I like us all hanging around together and that's going to stop if this continues between the three of us. Not to mention you and Fiona. Jesus this is like an episode of Jeremy Kyle. I think for the sake of our friendships we all just need to be friends.'

'I'm not pressuring you Ashton, but I'm not giving up that easy. If you chose Lucas then I'll be upset for sure but I'll accept it, if that's what you really want. But we will always be friends, no matter what.'

'Promise me.' I whispered.

'I Adam of the Druids of Bushmills, vow before our ancestors to always be a friend to Ashton of the Druids of Bushmills, of this I solemnly swear. So mote it be.' He said grinning at me.

'So mote it be.' I confirmed and smiled back at him.

He put his arm around my shoulders and we went back to the house. Friends again, for the moment at least.

When we got back to the house Lucas was downstairs eating breakfast with everyone else. He looked up as we entered, a curious look on his face but he didn't say anything, he just smiled at me.

'Want some breakfast?' Granny asked.

'Yes please Granny, I'm starving.' I said.

'Yes, I've worked up an appetite now.' Adam said smirking. I actually wanted to punch him, he was purposely trying to wind Lucas up.

Granny made us French toast covered with sugar. Mia, Leanne, Michael, Courtney and Emily had joined us for breakfast. Mum, Aunt Emma, Uncle Malcolm, Uncle Mark and Leona were all here too although they'd already eaten by the time we got back.

'Now that everyone's here, I should let you all know that I heard back from my contact. Sophia's last known location according to her phone was the Marine Hotel, that was 48 hours ago. So we can assume based on that information that she is still there. Whether she is being held captive or is there voluntarily we don't know. If no one objects, we will go tonight to try to either rescue her or convince her to come back with us. I think it would be best to wait until the early hours of the morning as there shouldn't be as many people around and we are less likely to be disrupted. We will go in groups of 4 or 5. Ashton, Adam, Lucas, Fiona and Mia will go in ahead of time to assess the situation and try to identify where in the hotel Sophia could be. Once they give the signal then Mia can get the message out to everyone that we are ready to go. Myself, Maureen, Leona, Malcolm and Mark will go in a car and Leanne, Michael, Courtney and Emily will go in another car.'

Everyone agreed. It was as good a plan as any when we didn't know what we were walking into, though I could help with that.

Granny pulled me aside separately. 'Ashton, you know what you need to do. Go ahead with Adam, Fiona and Lucas and let them search as spirits and Mia can help you watch over their bodies. Leave at midnight, we will leave at 1.30am.'

'Ok. I have plenty of reviver, I'll make sure to pack it all.'

'I think you should try to get some rest before then.'

'I will, but it's early yet, I will rest later.'

CHAPTER 18

I 'd spent most of the rest of the day in my room reading as a distraction, not only from what was about to happen this evening, but also the dilemma I was now in with Adam and Lucas. I liked Lucas but honestly I was still unsure if I could trust him and he could be really intense at times, but we had an undeniable connection. Adam on the other hand was my friend, he always made me laugh and I knew how much he cared about me. I now felt like I couldn't face Lucas, because I would have to tell him about what happened with Adam, and I just didn't feel like I could deal with any more drama right now. I had to focus on what was about to happen tonight.

Of course, the universe had other plans for me. A knock at my door drew my attention away from the book I was reading. 'Come in.' I called.

'Hey Ashton,' Lucas smiled at me poking his head around the door. 'Can I come in.'

'Yes I said you could didn't I?' I said rudely, immediately regretting my choice of words, but equally feeling annoyed that my hiding away like a coward and avoiding the uncomfortable situation that was about to happen, had came to an end. 'Sorry.'

'It's ok,' he said walking into the room and closing the door behind him. 'What's wrong? I came to see if everything is alright because you've been hiding away in here most of the day.'

I sighed and set my book down on the bed beside me. I looked up at him. 'Sit.' I said gesturing towards the armchair. He did as he was told. 'I need to tell you something. Adam and I kissed this morning.' I said getting it over and done with.

'Oh.' He looked thoughtful. 'Look Ashton, I can't say I'm happy to hear that, but it's not up to me who you kiss. We still don't know eachother very well, but I just can't seem to stay away from you or stop thinking about you. So as much as I don't want you to kiss Adam or anyone else for that matter, I've no right to ask you not to. Maybe Adam is a better choice for you and if that's the case then I'll not get in his way.'

'I don't know how I feel, I like you both. But there is just way too much happening right now I feel like this can't be a priority. I don't want to be dishonest or mislead either of you.'

'Ok, well I won't pressure you. I'll let you get back to your reading but I'll be downstairs if you need me.'
p
Well that went relatively well. I still had no idea what to do about either of them. This was a complication I didn't need right now.

I must have fell asleep at some point whilst pondering that, because the next thing I knew I was getting woke up by Adam tickling my feet.

'Oh my God would you stop it.' I said grumpily cracking one eye open. He cackled with laughter. 'What are you doing here?' I barked.

'It's 11pm, we're going to have to go soon, I thought I should come and get you.' he said.

'Ok, I'll get up. I guess I was more tired than I realised.' I said sitting up from where I was lying on top of the bedcovers.

'Is that why you've been hiding up here all day? Or have you just been trying to avoid me? He asked unusually serious.

'Probably more the second one.' I laughed and he laughed in response.

He sat on the bed beside me and put one arm around me. 'I don't want you to have to hide from me. I don't want to make you uncomfortable, just say the word and we can just go back to being friends and put the cat back in the bag.' I laughed.

'I'm not hiding from you, I'm hiding from the situation. Last night I was kissing Lucas, this morning I was kissing you, you both keep giving me these looks like you're expecting something from me and I don't know what I want. I'm confused and the more I see of both of you the more confused I get. I don't want to upset anyone, so maybe I should just stay away from both of you.'

'You know you can't stay away from me.' he said wiggling his eyebrows making me laugh again.

'I'm just afraid that whatever happens we won't still be friends. I'd hate that.'

'I promise, no matter what happens, I might sulk for a while, but I'll never not want to be your friend.'

I hugged him, his breath tickled my neck as he stroked the ends of my hair down my back. I lifted my head as he simultaneously lifted his and our lips brushed against one other, I sucked in a breath and before I knew what was happening I was kissing him. I ran my hands down his back, all the way down until they reached the hem of his t-shirt, lifting it up slightly my finger tips touched bare skin, I ran my fingers up his back as he pushed me back on the bed breaking our kiss and moving my hair to one side allowing him to kiss my neck, I moaned. I could feel my fire magic coming to the surface again and had to push it down. No one told you this part about being a druid. His hands roamed down my body, then I heard the door open.

'Ashton, oh my god *Adam*?' This was just perfect. It was Fiona.

We sat up and adjusted ourselves, I could feel the heat creeping up my neck to my face. I wasn't just embarassed, I was ashamed. Not twenty four hours ago Fiona had seen me kissing her brother, now she had found me in a compromising position with Adam, whom she had kissed only a few short days ago. What must she think of me.

Realising that neither me or Adam were going to speak, Fiona said crossly, 'I can't believe you would do this to my brother Ashton.'

'I'm sorry.' I said quietly.

'Somehow I doubt that. But that's not what matters right now. We have to go, I only came to see what was taking you so long.'

'I'll be ready in a few minutes. I'll meet you both downstairs.' I said nodding at Adam pointedly. He grinned back at me, only because he knew Fiona couldn't see.

They left and I tried to collect my thoughts and quickly adjusted my hair and shoved my trainers on and lifted my back pack, checking that the reviver was where I'd left it. I went into my walk in wardrobe and grabbed a purple zip up hoodie and put it on, then went downstairs to face the music.

Everyone was waiting in the kitchen. It looked like while I'd been hiding upstairs Granny or Mia had got in touch with everyone else and got them to gather here. Jacob and Anna were here now along with Shannon, Ryan, Macie, Diane, William, Daniel, Amy, Lyndsey, Rhianne, Liam, Andy, Graham and Michelle. The kitchen was pretty packed. Adam, Fiona and Lucas were also seated at the end of the dining table looking tense.

Granny gave me the last two bottles of reviver from the fridge and I put one in the pocket of my jeans the other in the pocket of my hoodie.

We all chatted in the kitchen, I made a point of avoiding Adam, Lucas and Fiona, talk about awkward.

As midnight approached I got more and more nervous, not just about what we were about to do but who I was about to do it with, both my kissing partners and my kissing partner's pissed off sister and a girl who hated me until her sister tried to have me kidnapped by the necromancers. Yay. What could go wrong?

When the time came we said our goodbyes and went out and got into my Range Rover. The mood was sombre, apart from Adam, and this was one time I could do without his cheerful attitude as it felt like he was gloating. I didn't know if Lucas knew about what had happened in my room a little while ago but he already knew about what had happened with Adam this morning, so Adam's good mood was making things awkward. Mia obvious sensed the atmosphere in the car. I was grateful she had sat in the passenger seat beside me.

'Did you all have a falling out or something?' she said quietly to me raising her eyebrows. Because of the silence in the car though every one heard it. I inwardly cringed.

'Or something.' I said.

Mia laughed.

Fiona decided to pipe up, 'I'm not surprised Ashton doesn't want to tell you. She's ashamed because she's been cheating on my brother with Adam.'

'I wasn't cheating on your brother, to be cheating on him we would actually need to be going out. Yes ok I kissed both of them but it's not like I've lied to either of them about it. So give me a break Fiona, I'm already feeling guilty about it.' I said.

Adam laughed.

'**Shut up Adam.**' Fiona and I said at once.

We all burst out laughing, breaking the bad atmosphere.

The rest of the journey was a little less awkward. When we arrived we parked on the road down the street from the Marine Hotel where other residents of the street parked their cars rather than using the car park at the back of the hotel.

'Ok, is everyone ready?' I asked.

'Can't wait.' Adam grinned.

'I'm ready.' Fiona and Lucas said at once in their creepy twin way making us all laugh again.

I lifted a bottle of reviver out of my back pack, wanting to keep the one in the pocket of my jeans and the one in my hoodie for emergencies. I knocked it back like a shot so not to prolong the god awful taste in my mouth. Immediately feeling energised. I nodded at Adam, to signal that he was going first.

I closed my eyes and reached for my black spirit magic, then carefully and gently pulled his soul from his body, taking the spirit out was the easy part, then I repeated the process with Lucas and Fiona. Adam hadn't stuck around to wait on them, he whooped loudly and zoomed off the second he was free, it was strange knowing I was the only one who could hear him. Fiona and Lucas left together, they had agreed to return before 1.30 am. Granny and the rest of the group planned on leaving at 1.30am.

That done, all Mia and I had to do was watch and wait. 'So you and Adam and you and Lucas.' she grinned at me. 'You get yourself into some interesting situations Ashton.' she laughed.

'You're telling me.'

'I overheard you talking to your Dad last night about the book of the Tree of Life. I heard about the book growing up, but no one knew where the book was. Have you heard the legend of The Giant's Causeway about Elara and Branwen?'

'Yes, Adam told me about it. Why?' I asked.

'The legends are wrong. My Mum used to tell me the stories, about how Elara and Branwen fought and formed the Giant's Causeway as it looks now. Branwen wanted to keep the Nexium for just the Druids, but Elara believed that the Druid's and the necromancers should work together and research the stone and use it to heal and protect their land. What they discovered though was that the Nexium could be used to invoke an additional power. Back then it wasn't unusual for Druid's to have more than one ability. Back then, Druid's and necromancer's married, procreated and so on. So Druid's are necromancers and necromancers are druids, we just have different abilities.

A Druid with necromancer abilities was known as a seer, but a necromancer with druid abilities was known as a Druid. Generally though a child born from a union of Druids and Necromancers were born with one or more Druid abilities, seers are rare, if a child born from a Druid and Necromancer didn't have any Druid abilities then their necromancy abilities seemed to be enhanced. But no one on record had ever had all 4 Druid abilities plus Necromancy abilities, until the Nexium. It was discovered by performing a ritual, the Nexium could draw out any dormant abilities. Most people the ritual was performed on gained an additional power, some gained two. Elara and her children gained the fifth power. They are the only Druids known to ever gain the fifth power which is a combination of Earth, Air, Fire, and Water from their Druid side and Spirit from the Necromancy side of their family. The book allegedly holds the ritual to invoke an additional power. That must be why the necromancers want it. Not only that but the ritual to invoke an additional power can strengthen the power they already have. So what I'm trying to say is, you must be an heir of Elara, if you can open that book.'

I sat in stunned silence for a second until a thought struck me. 'But how can that be? That book couldn't be over one thousand years old.'

'Elara and her children lived for a long time, they had the necromancer ability to prolong their lives. The book originates from somewhere around the 1500's and is imbued with magic so that only the heir can open the book, so no doubt there will be other protections placed on the book to preserve it.' Mia said.

'But it still doesn't make sense. The book said

The heir of our bloodline shall have the gift times five
Earth, Air, Water, Fire and Spirit.
Should they follow the path we set forth for them,

Our ancestors will bestow them with the coveted fifth power
Thus our line will endure.'

'What doesn't make sense? What the book says is exactly like I told you.' Mia said.

'But I already have all five abilities.' I said.

Mia looked sharply at me stunned. 'That can't be true. I knew you were more powerful than most and you have necromancer abilities but you can't have all five powers. It's just not possible.'

'Why is it not possible?' I asked.

'Because then the prophecy in the book is wrong. How could you be the heir if you already have the fifth power?'

'Maybe the prophecy is wrong.'

'Prophecy's are never wrong, they can be misinterpreted but not wrong.'

'Well then that's probably all it is, it's just been misinterpreted.'

'Yeah maybe,' she said but she didn't sound convinced. She zoned out deep in thought.

I stared out the window of the car wondering what it all meant. I couldn't be the heir if I already had the fifth power, but I'd already opened the book and only the heir could open the book. There was no use thinking about it now anyway. I checked the time. It was 12.52 in the morning, hopefully Lucas, Fiona and Adam would be back soon.

Fiona reappeared first, I didn't waste time talking to her whilst she was in spirit form as I knew Mia wouldn't be able to hear so I told her to get back into her body first then we could talk. While I was doing that Lucas also reappeared, so I reattached his spirit to his body too.

'Did you find her?' Mia asked as soon as they were both upright.

'Yes shes there.' Lucas said quickly. 'But it's not going to be easy to get to her. They have her tied up in the basement with special handcuffs that stop her from using her magic. There's only one elevator that goes to the basement level and it's guarded, there are also stairs which are guarded, another guard is placed outside of her room and another in the room with her. There are a lot of people inside the hotel, there seems to be a wedding going on. I don't know which are necromancers and which aren't, so that's going to make things tricky. I think we should go now. Text everyone the information of where she is being held and let's go.' he said.

Mia gasped when she heard that Sophia was handcuffed. 'We have to go.'

'Wait, what about Adam?' I asked. 'We arranged to go in at 1.30am with everyone else, I think we should wait.'

'Can I talk to you for a minute alone Ashton?' he asked.

I rolled my eyes but opened the car door and got out. He walked around the car to speak to me quietly. 'I didn't want to say this in front of Mia, but there is someone in the room with Sophia now, they are torturing her. If we wait for everyone else, god knows what they will do to her, or she could be dead.'

'Shit! What do we do? Where's Adam? We need him to get back to his body pronto.'

'I haven't seen him, he just took off like last time, doing his own thing. But his body is safe here in the car, no one knows we're here. Just lock the car, he will be fine.' Lucas said.

'I don't know, I don't feel right about this. But I also can't leave Mia in the car alone with him and I doubt she would stay anyway when she knows her sister is in there and by the sounds of it, it's going to take all of us to get past the guards.'

'I don't think we can wait Ashton. She didn't look good.' he said.

'For christ sake. Ok, we'll go. I opened the car door and spoke to Fiona and Mia. 'Send out text's to everyone to tell them not to wait, they need to come now. Tell them someone needs to come to my car to guard Adam's body and let them know where we've parked and that Sophia is in the basement. Then let's go.' I said.

'There's a fire exit at the back that has been left open from one of the security guards going for a smoke, it's close to the stairs to the basement. I think that's our best bet.' Lucas said and I nodded.

Mia and Fiona fired off the text messages and got out of the car. I took one last look at Adam's body and locked the car, feeling bad about leaving him without protection, but knowing we needed to move. I prayed that he would be ok. He would probably come back to his body and be pissed that I wasn't there to put him back together.

We walked down the street on the opposite side of the road to the Marine Hotel. When we were far enough away we crossed the road and made our way to the car park at the back of the hotel where the open fire exit was. Lucas entered first with me, then Mia and Fiona behind.

Suddenly Lucas hissed behind him 'Act like guests.' He put his arm around me and started talking loudly, 'We should go to the Giant's Causeway tomorrow to make the most of our last day here.'

Straight ahead I noticed a guard standing guarding a door. Lucas whispered 'Get ready.'

Fiona replied to Lucas, 'That sounds good.' in a loud but obvious voice drawing the security guards attention to us. I smiled at him as we approached, pulling on my air magic with every step, when we had nearly reached him I lifted my hand up as if to brush my hair back behind my ear and instead pressed my hand to his temple and zapped him with lightning. His eyes rolled back in his head and he instantly dropped to the floor.

'Nice one.' Mia said.

'We have to hide him before anyone sees. Open the door Lucas.' I said.

Lucas stepped over the guard to open the door, but there was a number lock. 'Shit, we need a code to get in.'

'Great, now what?' I asked.

'Can't you just zap the door too?' Fiona questioned.

'That might actually work you know. What do you think?' I asked Lucas.

'Do it, we don't have much time.'

I walked over to the number pad and pulled on my air magic and zapped the number pad with lightning. It smoked a little. I tried the handle, thank god it opened. I held the door open whilst Lucas dragged the guard into the small space at the top of the stairs. We all filed in and closed the door, then Lucas set the guard down and went ahead of us down the stairs. Expecting another guard at the bottom, we were surprised when there wasn't one, there was no lock on the door down here either. He turned left down the corridor.

'When we reach the end of this corridor there's another corridor, Sophia is in the third room on the left. There's a guard outside. Let me go ahead and deal with him, we need to be quiet so as not to alert the guard in the room with Sophia.' Lucas whispered.

We all nodded and followed along behind him until we reached the end of the corridor. Lucas, peered around wall then turned back around to us. 'Still just the one guard. Wait here but keep an eye out.'

He turned and walked down the corridor, 'Hey what are you doing down here?' the security guard.

'I was just looking for one of the bridesmaids, she told me to come back to her room.' Lucas said sounding drunk.

'Listen mate you're in the wrong place, I don't even know how you got down here, but you're not supposed to be here, you're going to get me in trouble.' the security guard said.

'She told me her room was on the bottom floor. This should definitely be it.' Lucas slurred again.

'This isn't the ground floor this is the basement level, you need to go.' the security guard was getting pissed off now.

'Ok ok my mistake. I'll just go back.' I peeked around the corner to see Lucas staggering in the opposite direction from where we came.

'Mate you're getting on my last nerve, you came from the other direction.' The guard said pointing his thumb over his shoulder.

'I didn't, I came this way.' Lucas argued.

'In the name of god, come on, I'll take you to the elevator.' The guard following Lucas up the corridor muttering under his breath.

'I guess that's our cue.' I whispered.

We sneaked down the corridor to the door that the guard had been standing in front of. Of course it had another keypad. I held my hand up and zapped the keypad. I put my fingers to my lips and waved Mia and Fiona to one side of the door and then I flung open the door and immediately flattened my back against the wall so I couldn't be seen.

'What the fuck.' a voice came from within the room. The owner of the voice stepped out of the room and turned his head to look right at me as I zapped him in the temple just like I did with the other guard. I stepped over him and into the room, unfortunately realising too late that there was another guard in the room. He struck me on the side of the head so hard that the room spun around me as I hit the floor.

'Ashton are you ok?' I could hear Fiona's voice as if it was in the distance.

I tried to sit up, but it was like an invisible force was dragging me back down. I could hear fighting going on around me, then I heard Lucas's voice then more footsteps and fighting. Lucas lifted me up. 'Lucas, get me the reviver from my pocket.' I wasn't sure if it would work but it was worth a try. He reached his hand into my hoodie pocket awkwardly because he was still carrying me and handed me the bottle. I opened it and drank. Instantly the fuzziness in my head cleared though it still throbbed. I reached my hand up to the side of my head and felt wetness and when I looked at it, it was coated in my blood. What the hell had that guy hit me with. 'Put me down Lucas, I'm ok.' He looked at me dubiously. 'Just do it.' I ordered.

He set me down on my feet. I was a little unsteady but I felt much better. I looked at the mayhem around me. There were three passed out necromancers on the floor. 'Where's Sophia?' I asked.

'She's safe, she's with Mia. We need to go.'

When we walked out into the corridor there were several more passed out necromancers on the ground. We stepped over them and ran down the corridor to the stairs and started running up them just as two more necromancers came down, Lucas pulled me behind him and shot his water magic at them knocking them off their feet. We ran up the steps past them but one of them grabbed me by the leg pulling me to the floor, I kicked him in the face, ouch, but its where my foot landed. I scrambled to my feet as Lucas helped pull me up by the hands. When we got to the top of the stairs we pushed out through the door and ran back down the corridor we had came in, to leave through the fire exit. Just before we reached the door, Granny came charging through it. 'Thank God you're ok Ashton, come on quickly.' she said waving us out. But there was a yell from behind me, I turned back and looked, regretting it instantly. There were 6 necromancers.

I heard another yell 'It's the girl, stop her.' We needed to run, I took another step and a smoky shadow appeared in front of me. It could only be a wraith. I tried to run through it, but it wrapped itself around me squeezing my rib cage until I felt like I was going to pass out. Granny was looking for an opening to blast it with her fire magic but she was afraid of hitting me instead. Lucas blasted it with his water magic, but only resulted in soaking me. Instead Granny stepped in front of me and started blasting the other necromancers, but the wraith didn't let go its hold on me. Lucas joined her, but another two wraiths appeared and wrapped themselves around Granny and Lucas. It wasn't looking good. But then it hit me, I was a necromancer so maybe I could control the wraiths. I closed my eyes to help me concentrate on anything other than the wraith squeezing the breath from my lungs and pulled on the now familiar strand of black spirit magic and pushed it towards the wraith, but nothing happened, I really needed to figure this shit out when

I wasn't in the middle of a life and death situation. I let go of my magic and instead focused my attention on the wraith and I pulled its energy into myself, like using my magic in reverse. It was working, it's grip on me was loosening, so I kept going and pulling until it completely disappeared.

'How is she doing that?' One of the necromancers said clearly terrified. Yeah you should be terrified because now I'm pissed off.

The necromancers were edging closer to me so I pulled on my air magic and blasted them all off their feet in one huge gust of wind and then turned my attentions back to Granny and Lucas, pulling the energy from the wraiths into myself as quickly as I possibly could before the necromancers regrouped.

Once they were both released I shouted 'Run!', and run we did. All the way out of the car park, across the road and down the street to where our car was parked and where everyone else was gathered with their cars near by. I was starting to feel woozy again. Those wraiths didn't agree with me.

'Where's Sophia? Is she ok?' I asked.

'She's here and shes ok.' Mia appeared from behind my Uncle Malcolm.

'Thank God, is everyone else ok?'

'A few are a little banged up, but everyone is pretty much in one piece.' Uncle Malcolm said.

'Well apart from Adam. He's probably chomping at the bit, waiting for you to reattach his soul to his body.' Mia said.

'Ok I'll go do that, does someone have room in their car to take Mia and Sophia back? We will meet you all at Granny's.'

'I do,' Leona said.

'See you all soon.'

I walked to my car, Jacob and Anna were waiting beside it. 'Hey thanks for watching over Adam.' I said

'He's not here Ashton.' Jacob said.

I unlocked the car and opened the back door where Adam's body had been, but the car was empty. 'Where is he?' I asked confused. 'Where's Adam?' my voice raised in pitch, I was panicking. I looked all around the car knowing he wasn't there but wanting to be thorough anyway. Lucas, Fiona and Granny were beside me in an instant. 'This doesn't make sense, he was here, he couldn't have got back in his body without me. Where the hell is he?' I said tears rolling down my cheeks now. 'My car was locked, how?'

'He was gone when we got here.' Anna said.

'Sorry Ashton.' it was Jacob.

My Granny put her arm around my shoulder. 'It's ok dear, we will figure this out. Sit down.' she guided me to sit down on the back seat of the car, my feet on the pavement. I was shaking. 'Ok Ashton, tell me what happened with Adam.'

'Lucas and Fiona found Sophia, the necromancers were hurting her, so we had to go help her and Adam hadn't came back yet, so we left him here, we just left him. We locked the car. I thought he would be waiting when we got back, but he's not here, his body and spirit are both gone. I don't understand where he could be, who would have known he was here.' I looked up and several other people had gathered around. 'Have any of you seen Adam?'

I demanded. 'He has to be somewhere.' I turned to look at Granny again. 'He must be inside, we have to go back in and look for him, we can't leave him here.'

'Ashton it's too dangerous, we're all exhausted and injured and most of our numbers have left. There has to be something we're missing. His body can't have got up and walked off.' she said.

I couldn't speak, I couldn't think, all I could do was feel, complete and utter heartbreak and guilt. My lifelong friend, gone and I didn't have a clue where to even begin looking for him. What if his body and soul were separated forever. I needed to snap out of it, I wouldn't give up, I wouldn't stop looking until I found him. I owed him that at least.

'What about if I send someone back in? In spirit form I mean. Just to see if he is there.' I said not willing to give up.

'I will look for him.' it was Lucas.

'Thank you.' I said swiping the tears off my face.

Granny nodded at Lucas and moved to let him pass her. I stood to let him sit down in the back seat again. 'I'm ready.' he said.

I felt for my spirit ability and used it to tug on his soul, his spirit popped out of his body and his head sagged. 'Be careful.' I said.

'I will.' he replied and he was gone.

I checked the time, it was 2.30 am. I prayed to God that he would find Adam. I don't know what I would do if he didn't. I could barely stand the wait, I paced up and down the pavement, only stopping to stare in the direction that Lucas had gone to see if he was on his way back. Eventually I sat down in the car and just stared blankly into space. I can't believe this was happening.

It was a nightmare, why did I leave Adam on his own. I knew I shouldn't have left him but I done it anyway.

Granny looked at me, 'Ashton, it wasn't your fault.'

'How did you know that's what I was thinking?' I asked.

'I just know. Just like I know Adam is ok. Wherever he is.'
'I hope you're right.' I said, then I seen the outline of Lucas's spirit returning.

'Lucas!' I exclaimed. 'Please tell me you found him.'

He shook his head sadly and I sobbed. Oh God. I needed to calm down so I could put his soul back in his body.

'Ashton, where's the reviver? You need to drink it, it will clear your head.'

'I have one in my pocket.' I said tears falling fast down my face. I reached into my jeans pocket and pulled the bottle out. I opened it and drank it barely noticing the disgusting taste. I felt the energy coursing through me, but I couldn't bring myself to care. Lucas sat down inside his body and I reattached his spirit.

'Did you see anything at all that might lead us to Adam?' Granny asked the second he lifted his head.

'I'm sorry, I didn't.' he replied.

'Ashton, we should go home. You need to rest, we will figure this out after you have got some sleep. You have expended far too much energy and you are injured and bleeding. You're no help to Adam like this.'

I just nodded feeling complete and utter dispair.

'I'll drive us back.' Lucas said.

Granny gave me a hug and went to her car, Uncle Malcolm left with her. Jacob and Anna both hugged me and left to go to their own cars.

I got in the back seat with Fiona. She put her arm around me and I lay my head on her shoulder. 'He will be ok Ashton.' she whispered. We stayed like that all the way back to Granny's house.

I couldn't bring myself to speak, or even face anyone when we got back. I knew Sophia was safe and I was glad, but I couldn't pretend I was happy when Adam was gone, so I left the other's and went to my room alone. I went into the bathroom and washed the blood from my face, wincing from the gash on the side of my head.

I took my clothes off and got into bed in just my underwear, pulling the blanket over my head and cried until I fell asleep.

CHAPTER 19

I heard a voice that I knew I recognised but I was so tired it wouldn't compute. 'Ashton, I'm here, I'm ok, wake up.'

I startled awake once I realised, that it was Adam's voice that I heard. 'Adam? Where are you?' I was met with silence. I turned the lamp on my bedside cabinet on and looked around my room but there was no one there. Realising that I must have dreamt Adam calling me, a sob built up in my chest again. Not only was I upset that Adam was gone and was likely in a lot of danger but I also felt guilty because I knew it was my fault. But I had to pull myself together because I was no use to him like this and feeling sorry for myself wasn't going to help anyone. I just needed to think what to do. Then just like that it came to me, something Mia had said the first time we had separated Adam, Lucas and Fiona's souls from their bodies at Dunluce Castle. She had asked me if there was something like a ghost call that we could use to call them back to their bodies. I don't know if there is, but there is someone who might know - Gavin. I had to find out. I didn't stop to think about what time it was, I just grabbed my phone from the charger on my bedside cabinet and scrolled through to quickly find Gavin's number and called him.

'Hello? Ashton? Is everything alright?' he sounded like I had just woken him.

I cringed when I looked at my phone and realised it was 5.27am. 'Sorry er Gavin,' I still didn't know what to call him. 'I didn't realise the time, but It's an emergency and I think you're the only person who can help, since you're the only necromancer I know.' I said.

'What do you need?' he replied.

I quickly explained to him what had happened. He agreed to come over right away, so I quickly got up and got a shower.

That done, I felt a bit more human, but I still felt groggy from my lack of sleep and probably a hangover from using so much magic the night before. So I decided to try and make myself a new batch of reviver, it was better than doing nothing while I waited on Gavin arriving. When I'd finished, I began pouring the reviver into bottles when I heard tyres on the gravel outside. I left what I was doing and ran to open the front door. The house was silent at this time of the morning, with everyone only going to bed a mere few hours before, I doubted anyone would rise anytime soon, well except maybe for Granny.

'Thanks for coming.' I said, as Gavin reached me he pulled me into a hug.

'I was happy you called, I'll do what I can to help.'

I stepped back from him and smiled, 'Thank you, let's go into the kitchen, I was just finishing up a batch of reviver, I feel like I need it.'

He followed me in and I finished bottling the reviver and put all but one bottle away in the fridge. I doubled the recipe this time so I would have twice the amount. I took a quick sniff of remaining bottle, confirming that it tragically smelt just as disgusting as it tasted so I must have got it right and I downed it quickly. I shuddered, but instantly felt a surge of energy.

'So, what do you know about calling back spirits after you have released them from their bodies?' I asked.
Gavin took a seat at the dining table, but before he spoke I said, 'Sorry, it's rude of me to ask you to come here at this time of morning and not even offer you a tea or coffee.'

He smiled at me, 'Don't worry Ashton, I understand that this is more pressing. We can think about coffee afterwards. To answer your question, I was thinking about this on my way over. There is a way to call a spirit back to their body but unfortunately Adam's body is gone, so that isn't going to work, but I had another idea. Very powerful necromancers were once able to pull the soul from a person's body from a great distance, so long as they have something personal belonging to that person and they have felt the person's soul before.'

'Thank God.' I said, relieved. 'Just tell me what I need to do.'

Gavin looked at me sadly, 'It's a bit more complicated than that Ashton. There is some danger involved.'

'I don't care, I will do whatever it takes to get him back.' I said vehemently.

'The danger isn't to you Ashton, it's to Adam. If you pull his soul from his body, there is no way to return it at a great distance, so you have to hope that Adam knows where his body is to allow us to find our way to it and reattach his soul, otherwise he could end up trapped as a spirit forever.'

'Shit, why is nothing ever easy.'

'The good thing is that we have time on our side. It's 6.30am, what time do you think Adam went missing approximately?'

Gavin asked.

'Between sometime just before 1am and 1.30am.' I replied.

'Great, that's good, that means he can't have got too far in five hours. So the sooner we get started the better.' Gavin said.

'Ok what do we need to do?' I asked.

Gavin gave me instructions, it seemed pretty straight forward, I just needed something belonging to Adam and although I didn't have anything that belonged to him, I did have something he gave me, which Gavin said would work. I rushed off to my room and found the jewellery box that Adam gave me with the pencil inside. I brought the whole box with me and grabbed my robe, and ran back downstairs as quietly as I could. Once I'd returned, I grabbed a few bowls and we made our way out to the field at the back of the house to gather offerings for my ancestors, then we made our way to the stone circle around the Blackthorn tree. I put on my robe and knelt on the ground. Gavin knelt beside me and helped me arrange my offerings to the ancestors.

'Are you ready?' he asked. I nodded.

'Ok, hold onto the personal item belonging to Adam and think of him and the essence of his soul and repeat after me;

I call upon our ancestors ,
Please accept my humble offerings as thanks
for your borrowed power,
Please aid me in my search for this soul and bring them to me.
So mote it be.'

I held the pencil between both hands and repeated after Gavin, but this time instead of a gust of wind, torrential rain, the earth shaking or flames exploding a ghostly figure of a man shrouded in a cloak appeared before us. I almost jumped.

'So mote it be.' the ghost said and then vanished as quickly as it appeared.

We waited quietly, but nothing happened. I looked at Gavin questioningly but he just shook his head. I could feel the despair creeping up on me again, I was close to giving up, then I suddenly seen something moving quickly towards us from beyond the blackthorn tree until it stopped abruptly in front of us. It was Adam. He looked around in shock.

'Oh Adam, thank God you're ok. What happened to you? We need to know where your body is so we can bring you back.' I said relief washing over me at the sight of him.

'Ashton, you're in danger. Are you and Gavin alone?' he asked, looking around as if he was expecting someone else to jump out at us.

'Yes it's just us. What's wrong Adam? Who done this?'

'It was Lucas, he's not who you think he is, he's a necromancer....'